An Irishman's Odyssey

J. Thomas Hennessey, Jr. PhD

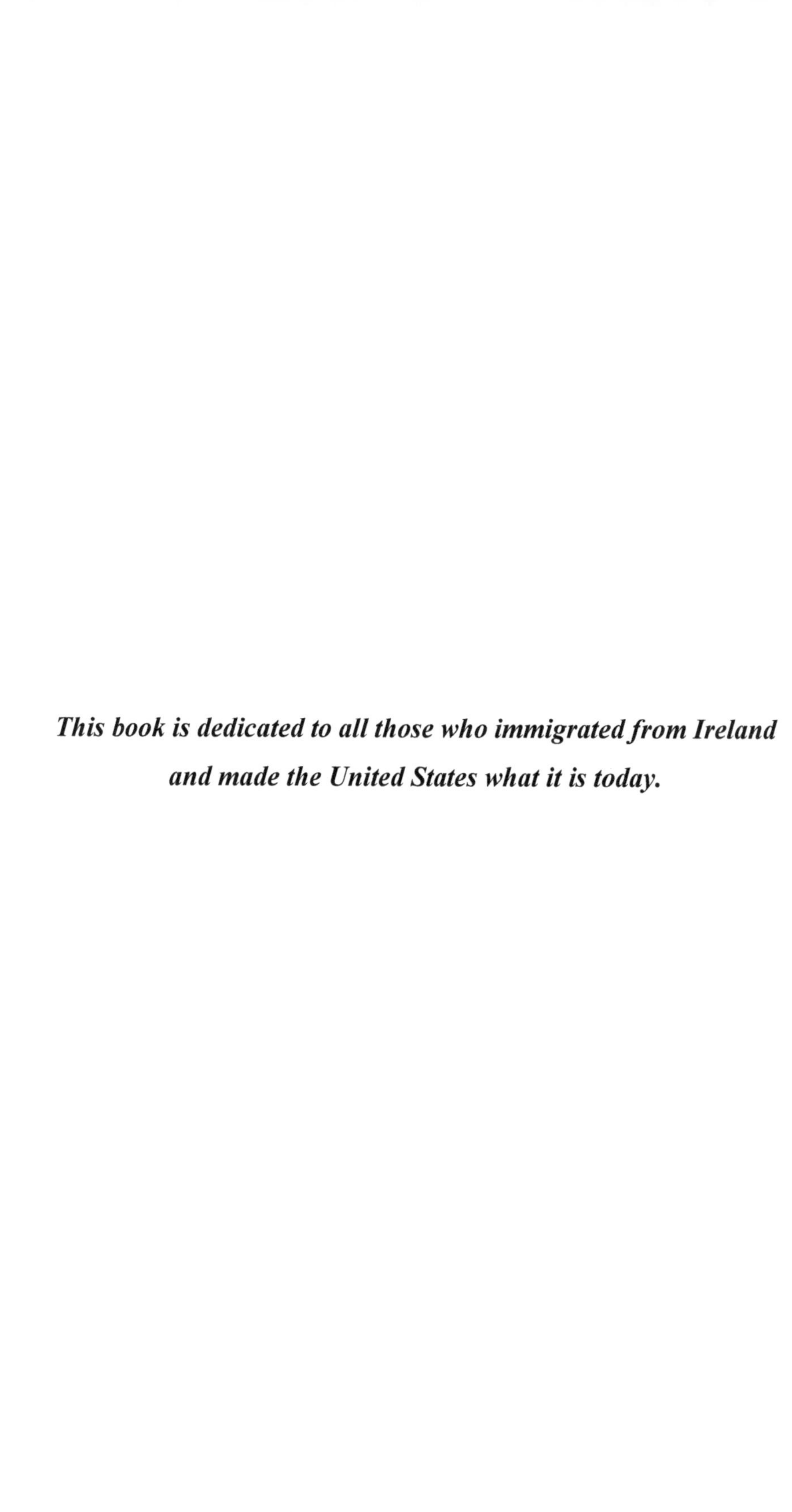

This book is dedicated to all those who immigrated from Ireland and made the United States what it is today.

Table of Contents

Chapter 1: The Beginning

It is 1832, and two fifteen-year-old youths, Liam Flaherty and Michael Nolan, are gathered around the hearth of a small stone cottage. Liam, the larger of the two, has a shock of dark red hair that matches his sometimes fiery spirit. Michael, with his dark hair and more reserved nature, provides a stark contrast to his lifelong friend. They are farmers, the sons of farmers, having spent their young lives working the land. Both young men, with their rough hands and solid physiques, reveal years of toil in the fields. It is early October, and a cold wind whistles around the door and windows. The small peat fire gives little warmth beyond the hearth.

Mrs. Mary Flaherty, the mother of one of the boys, has been a widow for five years. She married young, at fifteen, and had her only son at sixteen. Her beloved husband, Aidan, and Liam's father died of smallpox when Liam was ten. Since then, she and Liam have barely scraped by on the small farm left to them by Aidan Flaherty. She looks fondly at her redheaded son and asks. "Liam, will the harvest last us through the winter?"

The boy replies in a low voice, "Mam, it seems unlikely. We may have to buy some food stores until we can bring in a harvest in the Spring."

"Is your family as poor off as the rest of us, Michael?" says Mrs. Flaherty to the second boy.

"Aye, Mrs. Flaherty, we don't see our stores making it to the end of winter. Me father has yet to find more work."

To add to the shortage of food available to most poor Irish farming families, the imposition of the Tithe Act of 1823 required all occupiers of Irish agricultural holdings to pay monetary tithes instead of a percentage of agricultural yield to support the Anglican Church in Ireland. Most Irish farm families are staunchly Catholic and support the Catholic Church in Ireland rather than the Anglican or Protestant Church.

Protests against the Tithe Act have been mainly nonviolent. Few farm families pay the tithe, which the Constabulary collects, most of whom are Protestant. The Constables forcibly take from those who have not paid the tithe and, in many cases, leave the families destitute.

Michael, feeling the weight of the possibility of starving, looks at his lifelong friend and grimly states, "It's a sad, sad day, Liam. It seems that there is little comfort to be found in our homes anymore. We work the land, and more and more is taken from us. It is hard enough to work a poor piece of land without what we make from it being taken away."

Michael, choosing his words carefully, says quietly. "I have heard tell that constables from Kilkenny Town may come the five miles south to Widow Hankin's home and farm patch in Carrickshock to collect the tithe she owes. We are but a mile from Carrickshock here in Knocktopher. Would they also come to us? Most here in our small village have refused to pay the tithe. I believe all the folk of Carrickshock and Knocktopher are united against the tithe and the British constables who enforce it. What happens if they take our remaining funds? Surely, many of us will starve this winter."

For the past year, Liam has been struggling with how to respond to the Tithe Act beyond simply refusing to pay. As if an opportunity has now presented itself, Liam replies, "I say we spread the word in the county that the constables are coming. If we gather enough men to assemble in Carrickshock, we will be more than enough to persuade the constables to leave."

"Has this not been done before?"

"Michael, when have we learned when the constables will show themselves? They seem to appear at a farm and demand the tithe. There has never been time to alert the villages."

The two boys look at each other, realizing they are proposing something that has not been attempted before. The gravity of their decision hangs heavy in the air, a stark reminder of the harsh reality they face. Caught in the moment of enthusiasm, they have little consideration for any violence that may ensue. Liam looks at his lifelong friend,

"What say you, Michael? Can we do this?"

Without hesitation, Michael replies, "Aye, I believe we can. I will gladly visit all my neighbors here in Knocktopher. I also have family in Carrickshock. Before we go to Carrickshock to meet the constables, we should have our neighbors bring their hurling sticks. The constables will see that we mean to be strong. I will have my hurling stick, as I suspect it will be needed."

Mrs. Flaherty, having heard this kind of talk from the two boys before, says to both boys, "Lads, we may resist the tithe, but tread carefully. The magistrates and constables will surely punish those who resort to violence. I could not bear to have the two of you come to harm. You may outnumber the few constables in the county, but the constables have guns, and you have but your hurling sticks." Her concern for their safety is palpable, adding to the tension in the room. Mary Flaherty has finished school, is well-read, and has taught Liam all she can. He is one of the few in his circle of friends who can perform higher-level math operations, including addition, subtraction, multiplication, and division. The skills Mary Flaherty practices in her avocation as a midwife. This has made Mary one of the few learned women in the village.

"Mam," says Liam, "I have no ill will toward any of the constables, but what they do against us cannot be forgiven. If we take no stand now, what will happen in the future?" His words are not those of a reckless troublemaker but a young man who feels a deep sense of duty and responsibility towards his family and community. His passion for freedom from oppression is almost palpable. To her dismay, Mary Flaherty sees this too often from young Liam.

As a widow, Mrs. Flaherty has little support beyond that provided by Liam and the donations she receives from her midwifery. She also knows full well Liam will do what he thinks he must, even if he does not realize it threatens their livelihood. She can only hope that anything the boys decide to do will not bring them harm. The sense of foreboding she feels is as unwelcome as the October draft that seeps into their humble home.

Turning back to the fire, Liam Flaherty and Michael Nolan discuss how best to alert their neighbors in both Knocktopher and Carrickshock that the Protestant constables will soon attempt to collect the tithe. They agree on a plan that includes almost every home in the two villages being notified. Between the two, each village and neighborhood will be visited by one of them.

Early the following day, Liam and Michael travel from home to home around Carrickshock and Knocktopher, talking with other county folk. After two days of traveling around southern County Kilkenny, everyone they spoke with agreed that a stand against the constables should be taken if they appear at Carrickshock to enforce the tithe. Liam is energized by the responses he has received from his neighbors. He is both excited and apprehensive that this may result in a step toward freedom from the Tithe Act. I am doing a good thing, he says to himself. Surely, the constables will see how united we are and will not attempt to collect the tithe from Widow Hankins.

While Liam and Michael work to alert others who might join the resistance, 38 armed constables are dispatched from Kilkenny Town to Carrickshock to collect overdue tithes in that part of the county. A relative of Michael's in Carrickshock receives word the constables will soon be on their way south from Kilkenny Town, and on the evening of October 13, 1832, he travels to Michael's home to warn him. Michael goes to Liam's, and the two begin making the rounds to alert the villages surrounding Carrickshock.

Liam's and Michael's efforts result in a crowd of almost a hundred men and boys armed with clubs, pitchforks, and hurling sticks descending on Carrickshock in the late morning of October 14. Most in the group knew Liam and Michael as the two who had alerted them to the constables' plans. Liam and Michael find themselves on the outskirts of Carrickshock with an angry and resolute group awaiting the constables' arrival. Most in the group are teenagers like them, with but a few older, unmarried men.

As they wait in the late morning, Liam turns to Michael,

"Are you ready, Michael?

"I am. I have my hurley at the ready."

"Let us follow to the center of the village and await the cowardly constables."

Liam and Michael walk quickly to the center of the village in the front row of the group. The uncertainty of what may happen next is furthest from their minds. Their hope that the show of force by the villagers will deter the constables without violence is short-lived. As the group, now numbering a hundred or more, moves, Liam is filled with a confidence that stems both from his role in this demonstration and the number of those who have joined him and Michael.

An Irishman's Odyssey

In the early afternoon of Wednesday, October 14, 1832, 38 armed constables arrived at the village of Carrickshock. Much to the surprise of the constables, a large group of County Kilkenny and Carrickshock residents met the constables in the center of the village. The group shouted loudly that the constables should depart under penalty of a beating. The leader of the constables, Sergeant Jason Smyth, had not expected such resistance and, after some consideration, ordered the front five constables to fire their muskets over the heads of the crowd. His hope that the crowd would retreat with the threat of the musket fire is quickly dispelled as the larger crowd assaults the constables with clubs, hurling sticks, and pitchforks. To Smyth, it seemed like the musket fire had encouraged the crowd to attack rather than retreat. As the angry crowd descends on his detachment, he realizes he has seriously miscalculated the odds. He and his fellow constables now fear for their lives.

Liam and Michael, like those in the crowd, are initially stunned by the musket fire. Almost in unison, a roar from the group precedes a charge at the constables. Liam and Michael are carried along as the crowd quickly wades into the group of constables wielding their hurling sticks, clubs, and pitchforks. Liam promptly knocks down one of the constables and is shocked when he sees one of the constables impaled with a pitchfork by a boy of ten. Those five constables who fired were the first to suffer the onslaught as they failed to reload their muskets. The remaining constables could not fire their muskets with so many of the crowd now amongst them. The constables tried unsuccessfully to fight off the crowd, using their rifles as clubs. It became an uncontrolled melee, with anyone in a uniform the target of a dozen angry young men. Soon, five constables lay in the street, and the remaining thirty-three hastily retreated, carrying other wounded comrades. A few villagers suffered cuts and bruises, but a loud cheer rose as the constables, dragging injured ones, retreated. To the dismay of some of the villagers watching from their homes, five constables lying in the street are dead. The older men of the village know full well that retribution for their deaths will be swift and harsh.

While congratulating each other on their success in driving off the constables, many in the now rowdy crowd acknowledge Liam and Michael as the ones who rallied the crowd with their efforts to alert the villagers. In the Lion Inn, rounds of drinks were raised to celebrate the resistance's success. Until late in the evening, Liam and Michael enjoyed the spirit of the rebellion and complimentary pints, where they were hailed almost as heroes. As the two make their way home to Knocktopher unsteadily, they are in high spirits.

"We did it, Michael."

"Aye, we did, Liam. I wonder what is next? Surely the constables will come better prepared the next time.

On October 15, two wagons arrive in Carrickshock from Kilkenny Town to retrieve the bodies of the dead constables. As the bodies are collected and placed in the wagons, the wagon master, a former constable, visits the Lion Inn for a drink. During a casual conversation with others in the Inn, he learns two young men by the names of Liam Flaherty and Michael Nolan have been identified as the initiators of the assault on the constables. Upon his return to Kilkenny City, the wagon master reports to the constabulary the names of those he has learned were the key part of the resistance and may be responsible for the death of the constables. The following week, the local magistrate brands Liam Flaherty and Michael Nolan outlaws and places a bounty on their heads for their capture.

Within days, Liam and Michael learn of the bounty on their heads. They realize they must stay away from their homes lest the constables take them into custody. Liam's thoughts are now of his mother's concern and how she warned them about any violence. Before the constables could surveil his home, Liam sat down late one night with his mother. Liam described how they had successfully forced the constables to leave Carrickshock. Mary Flaherty was grateful her son was unharmed, but Liam's following statement was chilling,

"Mam, you were right. The magistrate in Kilkenny Town has branded Michael and me as outlaws. There is a bounty on our heads, and we know not what to do."

Mrs. Flaherty, shocked by Liam's statement, replies. "Oh, Liam. I was so afraid this would happen. I want nothing to happen to you. Go to the hills and stay away from home. Surely, the constables will come here to find you. Do not tell me where you will go so that I can truthfully tell the constables I do not know where you are."

"Mam, what shall we do? There are now no places in County Kilkenny where we are not known. Our efforts to tell our neighbors about the constables have made us known to most."

"Liam, when you can go to Father Murphy and seek his counsel. I know of no other person who can help. Be truthful with the priest, and he may be able to help." With those final words, she kisses her only son and sends him on his way.

Liam has stayed far away from his home in a small dugout in the hills for a week. He is cold, often wet, and miserable. Some nights, trusted friends place a meal or two in hidden locations that Liam can pick up after dark. Many times he wished he and Michael had never embarked on the dangerous effort to confront the constable. The consequences are now stark, for on November 20, 1832, the local authorities apprehended Michael Nolan as he tried to visit his family. After a long week in the Kilkenny jail and a short trial, a jury found Michael Nolan guilty of the murder of more than one constable on October 14th and sentenced him to be hanged. Upon learning of Michael's fate, Liam Flaherty knows he will receive the same. He remembers his mother's guidance and seeks help from his parish priest.

Late one night, just after Michael's sentence, Liam visits St. Michael's rectory and wakes Father Murphy by tapping on the window. Once inside, Liam tells the priest,

"Father, I am a wanted man. Michael Nolan has been sentenced to be hanged, and I will surely meet the same fate if I am captured. Can you help me?"

Father Murphy knows all about Liam and Michael's role in the resistance in Carrickshock. He has known Liam since birth. He sees a wet and miserable young man suddenly faced with the possibility of death by hanging. With some reservations, he decides to do what he can to help. He knows he is placing his own fate in the hope Liam will not be found and his role in helping Liam will not be discovered. The Catholic Church has objected to the Tithe Act, but harboring a convicted murderer has serious consequences.

"Liam, I may not pardon you for the sin of murder if you did so. The court's verdict may be incorrect, but you and Michael are likely to be held responsible for some of the injuries. If leaving Ireland quickly to avoid the same fate as your friend is the only option, then so be it. The Catholic clergy supported the opposition to the tithe, but we always hoped it would remain peaceful. There is little to be gained from violence, as it merely sows further violence. I have only a few shillings to provide for your travel expenses. Beyond that, a trip south to Cork and boarding a ship for another country is your best chance to avoid the same fate as Michael."

A very sorrowful young man replies, "Thank you, Father. I have no choice but to say farewell to family and friends in County Kilkenny. It will be a sad farewell, for I am certain I shall never see them again. Please tell my mother again that I never intended this to happen. It seemed the right thing to do, but it has turned out badly for all. Please give the shillings to her, for she will need them more than I."

Father Murphy assures Liam he will give his mother the message and the money. After providing some needed food and drink, he offers Liam one last blessing as he leaves,

"May God be with you, Liam."

With that, Liam leaves the parish with his small bag of belongings and stares down the road south to Cork. As the closest seaport, Cork is Liam's only hope to leave Ireland and avoid a trip to the gallows. The night is without moonlight as he must decide what to do next.

Chapter 2: Heading South to Cork

Liam expects the constables to have someone watching his home now that there is a bounty on his capture. As much as he wants to say goodbye to his mother, he can't risk being seen going to the house. With deep sorrow, for he is sure he will never see his mother again, Liam begins the long walk south to Cork by way of Grannagh. He begins his walk, but the night is short. Liam fears he will be seen and recognized if he stays on the road during the day. As dawn breaks, he finds a small thicket off the road south to Grannagh and falls asleep. It is a fitful sleep often interrupted by a chill wind. Exhausted, he sleeps through the dawn.

As the sun rises to midday, Liam awakens to the sound of a wagon heading south on the road. He leaves his hiding place and carefully approaches the road. Hiding behind a large tree by the road, He recognizes the wagon driver as a Carrickshock resident who celebrated the events of October 14 with others. Staying hidden as best he can, Liam shouts to the cart driver. "Is it you, Mr. Boynton?"

The driver stops his horse, "Aye, it is, and is it Liam Flaherty, the outlaw? Show yourself so that I may know you better."

Liam steps out from the tree, "It is me, Mr. Boynton. Is there room for me on the cart? I must make Cork before the constables find me."

"There is always room for one of the boys who stopped the constables at Carrickshock. I am on my way to Grannagh, so you can sit by me that far."

Mr. Boynton grabs Liam's hand and pulls him onto the seat beside him.

"Liam, we must be careful. Should we come upon someone on the road we do not know, you must hide in the wagon underneath the straw. Many know me along the way to Grannagh, but you are too well known amongst the constables. We will find Father Connor at St Mary's tonight and see what he can do to help you on your way."

The afternoon passes without incident, and the wagon arrives at Grannagh early in the evening and stops at St Mary's Church. Mr. Boynton goes inside and finds Father Connor alone in the sanctuary.

"Father, It's Paddy Boynton. I have a young man in my wagon who will indeed be hanged if the constables apprehend him. Can you help him get to Cork and find a means to leave Ireland?

Father Connor looks closely at Boynton before answering. "Were you at Carrickshock?

"Aye, Father, I was, and so was young Flaherty. We both protested the tithe on the 14th of October at Carrickshock. Only he and his friend were identified by the magistrate and are now convicted of murdering one of the constables."

"Bring the lad into the rectory after dark, and we will learn what is possible."

At full dark, Boynton leads Liam into the rectory and introduces him to Father Connor.

Father Connor looks at Liam and asks, "Did you murder one of the constables, Liam?"

"Father, I do not know that I murdered one of the constables, for we were wielding our hurling sticks about them, afraid at any moment they would fire on us. But, Father, I cannot say any blow I made was fatal to any of the constables. My friend, Michael Nolan, and I were in the midst of the crowd and may well have been identified that way."

Liam, I find your account to be honest and trustworthy. Why do you intend to go to Cork and leave Ireland?"

"Father, I have no confidence in the court and believe that should I be captured by the constables, my sentence will be death. So be it if I must leave Ireland to save my life."

Father Connor, as one of the more active priests against the Tithe Act, has a network of parishioners who share his sentiments. He is all too familiar with the courts in Ireland and finds Liam's situation one that requires his immediate support.

"Liam, here is what we shall do. You will stay the night here in the back of the rectory. I will be making the rounds in the village this evening. Many sympathize with the fate of the Catholic Church and oppose the tithe. There are also some willing to do more than complain."

Later that night, Father Connor visits two of his parishioners whom he knows to be ardent opponents of the tithe. Milo Finegan has a wagon he will use to transport Liam to Cork Harbor. The wagon is familiar to Father Connor, as Milo uses it to transport his illicit whiskey, or poitín, to customers throughout southern Ireland.

Angus O'Shaugnessy has a kinsman in Cork who is the mate on the Primrose, a four-masted freighter that carries cargo between Ireland and America. The priest prepares a letter from Angus to the kinsman on the Primrose, asking him to take Liam on as a crew member. Father Connor returns to the rectory and finds Liam sound asleep in the small room at the back wall. Father Connor knows that Finegan will be at the rectory shortly after sunrise, allowing Liam a few more hours of rest.

Before dawn, Father Connor awakens Liam with a mug of tea, a small loaf, and the plan.

"Liam, Milo Finegan will be here shortly in his wagon. He can hide you in the back of the wagon, as he often uses the wagon to move his poitín around the area. If all goes well, you should be in Cork by nightfall. Finegan will arrange a place for the two of you at an Inn close to the harbor. The two of you will be looking for a sailor named Michael Grogan. Mr. Grogan is the cousin of Angus O'Shaughnessy and master of a ship in the harbor. Angus has prepared a letter for his cousin, Michael Grogan. Milo will carry the letter to Mr. Grogan. It asks Mr. Grogan to take you on as a member of his crew. It says nothing about your plan to go to America. The Primrose, Mr.

Grogan's ship, travels from Cork to ports in America. Deciding how much to share with Mr. Grogan about your plans would be best. I can ask no more of Mr. Finegan."

"Father, I cannot thank you enough for all you have done. I would surely be in jail and likely sentenced to be hanged now had it not been for your kindness."

Liam, I am certain that your decision to leave Ireland was difficult. Travel beyond Ireland will not be easy for you, so take care during the journey. May the Lord watch over you."

When Milo Finegan knocks on the rectory door, Father Connor asks him in and introduces Liam.

"Milo, this is the young man I told you about last night. He is one of the many who opposed the Tithe Act in October at Carrickshock and did so with bravery. Unfortunately, the constables have branded him an outlaw, and he has no choice but to flee Ireland."

Milo Finegan looks at Liam. "Lad, it appears you have more courage than common sense. But never fear. Many in Ireland feel the same, and we will do what we can to keep you from harm."

Liam grabs his small bag of belongings and follows Finegan to the wagon. He then shows Liam the small false bottom of the wagon he uses to transport the illegal whisky, or poitín, around this part of Ireland.

"Should we encounter anyone we do not know, Liam, you will lie in the bottom of the wagon until we are clear. I will have you come out as soon as possible. It will be a mite uncomfortable, but a place no one will suspect, and we should avoid mishaps."

"Mr. Finegan, I am most thankful for your efforts and will do as you say."

At first light, Finegan and Liam are on the road to Cork. Liam sits out of sight in the back of the wagon, ready to lie in the hidden bed of the wagon as soon as he is told. Hours into the trip, Finegan tells Liam to lie down in the hidden bed of the wagon as he sees a group of men approaching. Liam quickly lies down in the false bottom and pulls the boards over himself. It is dusty and cramped, with only a few inches between his head and the boards. As the men approach the wagon, Liam listens intently to the exchange.

"Well, Well. It's Finegan, the poitín maker himself. Have you been making much?"

"Well now, Constable Hall, I may do that, but no more than I can drink myself."

"Would you have a little taste for us, Finegan?"

"I have but a little in this jug I was to have with me supper. I am happy to share with the loyal constables."

"You have always been a generous man, Finegan. We shall not forget your kindness."

After a short while, Liam hears the men leave. Finegan waits a few minutes and mutters, "Come on out, lad, those bastards have taken my jug and left me with none of my poitín. Or so they think. Hand me the jug by your feet."

Liam climbs from the wagon's false bottom and hands Mr. Finegan the jug he pulled from his hiding place. Finegan takes a small sip from the jug. In a voice dripping with bitterness,

"It's a sad day, Liam, when the constables take what they will whenever they like. It's a wonder we have anything left. I often wish I were there with you in Carrickshock to smash a few constables."

Liam and Mr. Finegan travel in silence for the rest of the day. As they approach the outskirts of Cork, Liam returns to the hiding place under the false bottom and waits to be told when they have arrived at the inn recommended by Father Connor. Although cramped in the small space, Liam falls asleep to the gentle rocking of the wagon.

Liam awakens to the gentle tapping on the boards above his head. As he joins Mr. Finegan at the front of the wagon, he can smell the ocean but cannot see it.

"Liam, we are at the inn nearest the harbor. We hope to find O'Shaughnessy's kinsman, Michael Grogan, here. I will put the wagon in the alley behind the inn. Keep in the wagon for your safety until I come for you."

"Thank you, Mr. Finegan. I shall do as you say."

Finegan enters the inn and finds it crowded with men. From their dress and their speech, he recognizes them as sailors. He orders a pint and sits at a small table, watching the men around the room. He looks for one sailor who might be in charge of other sailors. After a while, one man appears to Finegan as one who commands respect from the others. Once he overhears one sailor refer to the man as Grogan, Finegan knows he has found O'Shaughnessy's kinsman. Finegan leaves the inn and returns to the wagon. He taps lightly on the side of the wagon and calls softly to Liam.

"Lad, find me a small jug of the poitín. I have found Mr. Grogan and will be gifting him the poitín from his kinsman, O'Shaughnessy. I must come to know him better before I give him the letter about you."

Finegan returns to the inn and goes to the table where the man he believes to be Michal Grogan sits with two others. As he approaches the table, he says, "If you be Michael Grogan, I have a small gift from your cousin, Angus O'Shaughnessy," and places the small jug of poitín on the table. Michael Grogan looks up at Finegan. He sees a small, thin man who is obviously not a sailor. He then looks at the jug and says,

"What be your name, and how might you know that mean bastard, Angus?"

"Aye, Mr. Grogan, my name is Milo Finegan, and Angus and I have much in common. That small jug is some of the finest poitín Angus and I share on more than one night."

Grogan pulls the stopper on the jug and takes a small sip. The smile on his face lights up the room, and he exclaims,

"Angus has always had good taste in poitín, and I will savor this gift. What brings you to Cork, Mr. Finegan, other than greetings from that scoundrel cousin of mine?"

Finegan hands the letter from O'Shaughnessy he has been carrying and replies, "When you can, Mr. Grogan, take the time to read this letter from your cousin, and I will be ready to fulfill my part of the agreement. It should be done before morning if you are willing."

Grogan takes the letter, skims it, and then turns to his two table mates, "Lads, give Mr. Finegan and me a moment to take care of family business."

Finegan and Grogan are now alone at the table. Grogan turns to Finegan,

"Finegan, what my cousin asks of me is both dangerous and difficult. I would guess the authorities are pursuing the lad, and it is the reason for this means of communicating."

"Aye, it is a delicate question, Mr. Grogan. This lad was one of the leaders of the uprising against the Tithe Act in Carrickshock in early October. The constables are seeking those they believe are responsible for the slaying of the five constables on that day. They have identified only two. One has been apprehended and sentenced to death by hanging. The lad is the second. Surely, he will be hanged once the constables have their hands on him. The catholic priests have given the lad absolution and supported his leaving Ireland. Father Connor has helped your cousin prepare the letter you have."

"Finegan, before I agree on this matter, I must meet the lad and decide if I can take him aboard my ship. I have a room at the back of the inn. Get the lad up there and wait for me to join you. I will have the door open for you."

"Thank you, Mr. Grogan. I shall have the lad at your room within the hour. Regardless of your decision, the part of the agreement I have made with the church is complete. The lad either goes with you or finds his way in Cork or elsewhere."

Finegan and Grogan have another sip of the poitín, and Finegan bids a loud farewell to Mr. Grogan, which others in the inn acknowledge. Grogan responds with a hearty thanks for bringing the gift from his cousin. From all appearances, the two have parted ways for the evening.

Finegan leaves the inn and goes around to the back of the building. Tapping lightly on the bed of the wagon, he awakens Liam.

"Lad, I have given Mr. Grogan the letter from his cousin. He will see you in his room later this night. He will only decide if he can take you aboard his ship after meeting you. You must know should he not take you aboard, I will no longer be able to help you. I made the agreement with the church to bring you to Cork and deliver the letter to Mr. Grogan. The rest is up to you."

"I understand, Mr. Finegan, and I thank you for all you have done. I shall do my best to convince Mr. Grogan to take me aboard."

"Well, Liam, it might help, but I found Mr. Grogan a solid man who does not suffer fools. It would be best to convince him that you would be a boon to him, not an inconvenience. Once the door at the back of the inn is unlocked, we will make our way up the steps to Mr. Grogan's room. After Grogan returns, I will leave you there."

Finegan sees a light at the door closest to the wagon within the hour. He alerts Liam, and the two of them hurry up the stairs to the room at the back of the inn. Once inside the room, Finegan lights a small oil lamp. The two of them await Michael Grogan.

Just as he is about to fall asleep, Liam hears footsteps approaching the room. As the door opens, Liam sees a large man, ruddy in complexion with a short beard, enter. Liam springs to his feet as the man reaches for the oil lamp and turns it up to brighten the room.

Finegan turns to Michael Grogan, "Mr. Grogan, this is Liam Flaherty, the lad described in the letter from your cousin."

Grogan looks at Liam closely. He sees a young man of slightly larger build than most with dark red hair. His dress and shoulders tell of many hours spent working in the fields. He is no sailor.

Grogan turns to Liam, "How old are you, lad?"

"I am sixteen, sir," lies Liam.

"Can you read and do your numbers?"

"I can, Sir. I have finished school in my village."

"Now, tell me why you must leave Ireland in such haste. I will ask Mr. Finegan to vouch for anything you say to me."

"Mr. Grogan, my mate, Michael Nolan, and I went to Carrickshock when we heard the constables would take the widow Hankin's home and farm patch for unpaid tithes. The folk in County Kilkenny are opposed to the Tithe Act and have been rebelling by refusing to pay it. For the first time, we learned that the constables were going to forcibly take the tithe from a widow and leave her and her children destitute. We gathered with a large group of others from County Kilkenny. When the constables arrived, we warned them not to advance on the village. Instead, they fired on us. Before they could reload, many of us fell on the constables with hurleys and pitchforks. Before we knew it, a number of the constables lay in the street, and the rest retreated to Kilkenny Town. I know not that I may have killed any constable, but I confess I did swing at many with my hurley. My best friend, Michael Nolan, has been apprehended by the constables. He has been tried and found guilty of murder and is to be hanged before the end of the month. Surely, I will suffer the same fate when the constables find me. The Church has told me I had best leave Ireland."

Grogan turns to Finegan. "Mr. Finegan, does what the lad says match what you know?"

"Aye, it does, Mr. Grogan. It is as I have learned from many others. It is a sad day when two young lads are the only ones the constables want to find and hold accountable for the death of their comrades. I am told the crowd at Carrickshock numbered almost a hundred men and boys."

Grogan then turns back to Liam. "Lad, can you pay for your passage?"

"I have but a few coins left from my home. I do not know how much my passage might be, but I am a hard worker and can do whatever you require of me for the passage," replies Liam.

Grogan turns to Finegan and tells him his work is done, and he may leave. As Finegan goes out the door, he turns to Liam and offers his hand, "Good luck to you, lad."

"I thank you, Mr. Finegan, for all you have done for me. I shall not forget it."

As the door closes on Finegan, Grogan turns to Liam, "Lad, I will tell you my decision in the morning. You may sleep outside the door. No one will disturb you until I awaken. Then, over breakfast, I will decide and let you know."

"Thank you, sir. I look forward to the morning."

Liam bundles up his small belongings and lies outside Mr. Grogan's door. Unsure as to what Mr. Grogan will decide, Liam falls asleep quickly. Grogan is unable to sleep and ponders the issue presented to him. Should he harbor a young man wanted by the authorities? What are the consequences for him, his crew, and his ship? Although he does not own the Primrose, he operates her as though she were his. Even if the authorities do not find out he is harboring a fugitive, what will happen if the owner of the Primrose finds out? Finally, if he does not agree to take Liam on board as crew or passenger, he will eventually be apprehended and almost certainly meet the same fate as his friend. As Grogan falls asleep, he has not yet concluded that denying the lad is an eventual sentence of death.

Liam awakens as he hears Mr. Grogan moving about his room. He sits patiently until the door opens. Liam springs to his feet and greets Mr. Grogan with, "Good morning to you, sir."

Grogan looks at Liam speculatively and replies, "Join me at a table below, and I will share a morning meal with you."

Liam follows Mr. Grogan down the front stairs and sits with him at a small table in the back of the inn. Few are in the bar area as it is still early in the day. A small boy comes to the table and asks if they want something to eat. Grogan replies, "Bring us a bowl each of porridge and some of your mother's strong tea."

Looking closely at Liam and almost against his better instincts, Grogan makes up his mind, "Lad, I will take you aboard the Primrose as a crew member. The deck crew always needs hands on the sails. You should understand that this is a difficult and sometimes dangerous employment. You will be granted no favors aboard the Primrose, and some crew may resent you. It is up to you to make yourself a valued member of the crew. Should you fail to do so, I will leave you at the first port of call, and it matters not to me where that may be. Do you understand?"

"I do, Mr. Grogan. I shall not let you down."

"After your meal, make yourself scarce until the next morning. The crew will be on the docks at first light. We will load cargo for Liverpool, and then goods from Liverpool will be transported to America. I must add you to the crew list. So, what name shall we call you?"

Liam is recognized as a wanted man, Grogan cannot list him as a crew member under his real name. Knowing his friend will be hanged in Kilkenny, Liam replies, "It shall be Michael Nolan."

"So be it, Michael Nolan."

Chapter 3: Off to Sea

After a restless night sleeping just outside the town, at dawn Liam makes his way to the docks. Unsure which ship Primrose is, he asks a young man sitting astride a pile of logs where she may be. The young man looks at Liam, squints, and replies, "Aye, landlubber, she is right in front of you. Can you not read the lettering on her stern?"

Not the best introduction to a likely crew member, Liam blushes and says to the young man, "Mr. Grogan hired me just a day ago. I was to meet here to load freight for Liverpool. My name is Michael Nolan."

The young man smiles, "Michael Nolan, you are where you should be. Mr. Grogan and the rest of the crew will be here shortly. The large mound of timber, vegetables in crates, and slabs of marble you see along the dock must be aboard before the ship can leave on the evening tide tonight. Have you ever shipped out of Cork?"

"I have not. Life at sea has always drawn me; this is my first chance to join a crew." The white lie causes only a slight pause for Liam.

"You are fortunate, Michael. The Primrose is a good ship, and Mr. Grogan is a good master. My name is Jamie Watkins. I have sailed with Mr. Grogan since I was a wee lad, and now, at seventeen, I am a full member of the crew. Our pay depends on the cargo and the route we sail. After the owner and the mate receive their shares, each crew member receives their pay depending on their time with the ship and job. I am a deckhand, as you shall be, but my pay will be larger than yours, for I have made the voyage on the Primrose three times. Not all the crew may be as welcoming as me, for the more crew, the smaller the pay for each."

"I understand, Jamie. I must learn my tasks quickly. As deckhands, who gives us orders?"

"That is the man you dare not cross. Bos'n Adams is not a cruel man, but he brooks no laggards and drives the crew hard, especially the deckhands manning the sails. He has never lost a man, which for us on the sails on a stormy night is all the better for it. Here they come now. You had best be ready for some hard work."

Liam sees a large group of men led by Mr. Grogan and another larger man with a heavy beard. As they approach, Mr. Grogan gestures for Liam to come forward. Grogan then turns to the other large man and points to Liam, "Mr. Adams, I have hired this lad for the company. He has little knowledge of the sea but seems a strong lad. I leave it to you to employ him as you see fit."

Bos'n Adams looks askance at Liam and exclaims, "Could there not be more experienced sailors for the Primrose? I have little time to teach the lad what he needs to know."

Standing behind Adams, Jamie Watkins says, "Bos'n Adams, I will teach young Michael what he needs to know. He will be in the topsail riggings before we leave Liverpool."

"Young Watkins, you have made a tough choice. I fear you may lose that proposition when the red-headed lad falls into the sea. We need discuss this no longer. The cargo will be loaded as quickly as possible. You two lads, get a move on and take the logs aboard."

For the next four hours, with only a break for a quick pint, Liam and Jamie work with the crew members, hoisting loads of logs aboard the Primrose. Using hoists rigged from the yardarms, the remainder of the crew loaded the crates of vegetables and slabs of marble. Bos'n Adams instructed those carrying each load, be they logs or marble, exactly where to place them in the hold. As Liam watched the crew, he realized they were comfortable working together, and before he knew it, the Primrose was loaded.

Liam asked Jamie, "Why is Bos'n Adams so careful placing the cargo?"

Jamie, wiping his brow, scowls and replies, "Michael, can you not see?" The cargo must be balanced in the hold because an unbalanced cargo will endanger the ship and slow it down in the water. You have much to learn about the ship and the sea. Follow me forward with your bag, and I will show you where we sleep."

The next hour is spent with Jamie going over the Primrose. As a three-masted, square-sail merchant ship, each mast has a series of yardarms on which the sails are secured. Jamie points out the main mast in the middle, the mizzen mast at the stern, and the foremast in the bow. Liam looks at the five yardarms on each of the three masts and realizes the rigging is intended to be climbed to each yardarm. He turns to Jamie and, with some trembling in his voice, asks,

"Are we to climb to each of those cross pieces?"

Jamie smiles, "Aye, my Irish friend. We climb those and release the sails when the Bos'n gives the word. Stay close by my side as we climb, and I will show you how it's done. This shall be your first day of school as a deckhand."

With that, Jamie leaps on the first set of rigging, turns to Liam, and says,

"Climb with me, Michael. Dunno look down, keep your eyes on the topsail, and let your feet find the ropes."

Liam clumsily places his right foot on the ropes and is envious as Jamie scampers up the rigging to the first yardarm. Once there, he motions for Liam to come up and join him. Liam is slow to move up the rigging and often loses his grip or finds his boot slipping through. Out of breath and perspiring, Liam joins Jamie on the first yardarm of the main mast. James smiles and says,

"Looks easy, does it not? Now, grab the yardarm, put your feet in the rigging below, and follow me out on the yardarm. Michael, it would be best if you left your landlubber boots on the deck. Bare feet work best on the lines."

Liam looks down, realizing he is now twenty or more feet above the deck, and there are three yardarms above him. Swallowing, he follows Jamie out on the yardarm. "What is it we do with the sails?"

"See the ropes securing the sails? We use a bowline knot to hold the sails tight to the yardarm. When the bos'n shouts, 'Loose the sails,' we pull the knot, the sails fall, and the ship can catch the wind. As the yardarms are smaller the higher the mast, the fewer bowlines there be."

To Liam, it all looks so complicated. He can't imagine how he will be able to accomplish the tasks described by Jamie. Even as Jamie scampers up to the next yardarm, Liam calls out,

"Jamie, how can I do this if I cannot even keep my balance?"

"Once you have climbed the rigging many times, I promise you will be able to do it."

With that final reassurance, Liam and Jamie descend to the deck and continue Liam's introduction to what will be his home for the next five months. The crew members sleep in the forecastle (fo'c'sle), the section at the ship's bow where they hang hammocks to sleep in. Jamie introduces Liam to others in the berthing deck. All the younger crew members are short and wiry and seem no older than Liam. Many offer only perfunctory greetings when introduced. A distinct age gap is apparent to Liam as the older crew members are more than 10-15 years older than the others. The names of those introduced by Jamie are a blur until a prematurely bald, older sailor thrusts his face into Liam's and snarls,

"And who do you be? Are you some sorry Irishman here to take away honest coin from Englishmen?"

"My name is Michael Nolan, and while I am indeed Irish, I shall be your shipmate, like it or not."

"Steer clear of me, Irishman. I have no love for the Irish and their ways." He turns back to his small bag of belongings.

Jamie and Liam leave the fo'c'sle and return to the deck as the last bit of loaded cargo is repositioned in the holds.

"Michael, never you mind Turnbull. He is a poor sailor and an even poorer human being. I learned early to avoid him when I can and never, never go aloft with him. He might accidentally help you off the yardarm. We cannot prove it, but a young sailor went overboard from the topsail when he and Turnbull were tying off the sails. Turnbull claims the lad lost his footing, and there was no way Turnbull could help him. Others claim Turnbull pushed the young man, but the bos'n and the mate could not find out Turnbull pushed the lad."

As the Primrose made its way across the English Channel to Liverpool, Liam embarked upon the hardest, physically and mentally, five days of his young life. Ascending the rigging was but one of the tasks he had to master. His body soon adjusted to the rigors of climbing and pulling on the rigging and the sails. Learning the many ropes and knots essential to a seaman was a challenge. Fortunately, he quickly learned, and Jamie proved to be an excellent teacher. Over the week, the two became fast friends, and Liam sometimes forgot his now-dead friend, whose name he uses.

Still a novice seaman, Liam felt he might become a valued crew member once Liverpool Harbor was in sight from the topsail. His first sight of Liverpool Harbor on the evening of the seventh day was one Liam never expected. The small anchorage in Cork did not prepare him for the vast number of ships of all sizes and types that filled the harbor. His wonderment was interrupted by the Bos'n's call to "reef the sails." Along with the other young seamen, Liam scrambled up the rigging, grabbed handfuls of sail, and quickly secured them to the yardarm.

Having paid no attention to how the Primrose left Cork harbor, Liam learned quickly sailing ships do not maneuver well in ports. He soon heaved on ropes tied to heavy poles that slowly moved the ship toward the pier. As the ship closed to the pier, an older seaman threw a long rope to a waiting man on the pier. The pier man quickly secured the rope to a stanchion, and Liam and other crew members pulled the ship to the side of the pier. Just as he thought his hard work might be over, the Bos'n called for the work parties to begin unloading the cargo.

"Make quick work of it, lads. We have cargo to load and want to make the morning tide."

Quickly, hoists were again rigged on the mainsail's yardarm, and the crew began lifting the timber and granite cargo to the shore and into waiting wagons. The line of wagons with the cargo was soon loaded and away, when another line of wagons pulled alongside the ship. These wagons were loaded with large and small crates. As one of the few crew members who could read, Liam noticed many crates were labeled as fine furniture and others with gunsmith markings. As Liam and Jamie moved some smaller crates in the cargo hold, Liam asked,

"Jamie, is this a cargo the Primrose often carries?"

"Aye, it is. We carry furniture and guns to America on almost every crossing. We return with cotton and other materials."

"How long shall we be here in Liverpool, do you think?"

"I doubt we shall be here much more than the night. We must load the cargo for America and get the stores aboard for the voyage. We must have enough to feed us for two months or more, which will take to get the ship to America."

A little surprised, Liam exclaims, "Months at sea? Is America that far away?"

Jamie chides his friend and replies, "Where did you study your geography? It once took us more than two months to reach New York, but the winds were not in our favor for most of the voyage."

"Do you know where we are headed in America?"

"I heard the Bos'n talking with Mr. Grogan, and they said the city of New Orleans more than once."

"And where might that be?'

"It is somewhere in the south of America. Where exactly, I do not know. But I heard tell it is a wonderful place for sailors, as some of our older shipmates have been to New Orleans. They tell many stories about the drinking places and the ladies found there."

Chapter 4: Arriving in America

The Primrose left Liverpool on the morning tide and sailed south. It captured the trade winds west of the Canary Islands, which carried the Primrose southwest. After three weeks aboard the ship, Liam is now considered a capable crew member and has gained the confidence of Bos'n Adams. He may not be as proficient as Jamie, but he has learned quickly, and only occasionally does the Bos'n have to rebuke him for being slow on the sails. Liam has heeded Jamie's warnings about Turnbull and avoids him as much as possible, mainly when he is aloft. The Primrose is a well-run ship, and Liam spends his time aboard learning more and more about how she functions. Other than when they are aloft to trim the sails, Liam and Jamie spend time on the deck working on the many lines that operate the sails and mending any rigging.

By the end of the first four weeks, the crew had exhausted the fresh food supplies, and they now subsisted on salt beef, onions, hardtack biscuits, and the few fruits rationed to prevent scurvy. Now a tanned and muscular young man, Liam is one of the first up the rigging when the Bos'n calls for changes in the sails. Fortunately for the crew, the trade winds held, and the ship made good time. At the end of the sixth week from the topsail, Liam sees a small smudge on the horizon and yells to Jamie,

"Is that America to starboard?"

"Nay, I heard Bos'n Adams say it's what we call the Indies. He said we may yet be a week from making landfall in America."

Mr. Grogan expertly navigates the Primrose northwest between the Florida Keys and Cuba into the Gulf of Mexico. The seas in the Gulf are gentle, and Liam finds himself enjoying the smooth sailing. The days crossing the Gulf are spent with Jamie and Liam discussing what they might find in New Orleans. Soft winds from the south continue to push the Primrose north to New Orleans. By the end of the sixth day, the low line on the horizon becomes a clear landmass, and the crew of the Primrose prepares for landing in New Orleans.

The port of New Orleans is larger than the port of Liverpool but has fewer ships at anchor or at the piers. The young crew members launch a longboat to pull the Primrose to the dock. Unlike Liverpool, the port of New Orleans has not installed anchor points from which ships can pull themselves into port. To reach the piers, ships must provide their own power to their docking station.

Liam and Jamie scrambled aboard the longboat and grabbed an oar each. Primrose was slowly pulled to the pier as they and two other crew members pulled on their oars. After securing the ship at the dock, Mr. Grogan immediately went ashore to find the agent who would take charge of the cargo and ensure its delivery to the parties who had purchased the items. Having arrived late in the afternoon, Bos'n Adams and the crew are eager to unload their cargo. The crew begins rigging the hoists to lift the cargo from the holds and prepares to receive the provisions for their return voyage. They know they will be in port for at least a day and look forward to enjoying the city that so many have heard about.

The look on Mr. Grogan's face upon his return does not bode well for the rest of the day. The entire crew can overhear his loud voice: "What lunatic arranged for this cargo? The shipping office has no record of us arriving with cargo for someone they have never heard from. I must contact someone else to find an agent to accept our cargo. I will also have to arrange for us to load the cargo at the pier. We may be here far longer than I want." With that, Mr. Grogan goes ashore, finds a cart for hire, and heads to the city's center.

Crew members who have been to New Orleans before smile, knowing their time in the city will be longer than expected. Those who have never visited New Orleans now wonder what the town may offer with this extended shore time. The crew waits for Mr. Grogan to return with information on when the cargo can be unloaded. Liam and Jamie go to their hammocks and find what they can wear ashore among their belongings. Liam realizes he must plan how to leave the ship for good and make his way in America. With much regret, he will have to say goodbye to Jamie. He quickly puts that thought aside as the Bos'n calls the crew to the main deck.

"Seaman, Mr. Grogan has to make arrangements for the transfer of our cargo. We do not know when that might be, so we must wait for his return. Until then, we have much to do to prepare the Primrose for return to Liverpool. Should we be able to unload our cargo today and load the next load of cargo, we may stay the day. If Mr. Grogan says we must delay the unloading, I will allow half the crew to go ashore for a half day and the other half for the remainder of the day. Until then, we shall work on repairing sails, rerigging the shrouds, and preparing for unloading and loading."

As the day drags on and Mr. Grogan has not returned, it is evident the cargo will not be unloaded soon. A weary and disgusted Grogan returns to the Primrose as night falls on the port. He sees the ship is prepared to both unload its current cargo and load the cargo at the pier. The sails are neatly furled. Ropes, some with new cleats, are coiled and ready for us. The deck is clean, and the sailors are now a much cleaner-looking lot than when he left. He stands on one of the port-side lifeboats and addresses the crew.

"Lads, the agent responsible for receiving our cargo has had a misfortune. I have had to find another agent who will arrange for the cargo to be transferred to a warehouse. Unfortunately, that agent was not able to arrange for wagons until Thursday. As it is now Tuesday, we will remain here until then. Bos'n Adams will establish the watch for the time we are in port. I will pay each crew member a partial payment of his wages so you may have some coin ashore. For those who have never been to New Orleans, I warn you, there are many ready and able to take your wages before you know they are gone. Watch yourselves and be ready to transfer the cargo at first light on Thursday. Bos'n establish the watch."

Once the crew's watch responsibilities are established, Liam and Jamie assemble outside the Master's cabin to receive some of their wages. They look each other over and smile.

"We look like fine young gentlemen, do we not, Michael?"

"My feet do not like my boots as they once did. Why is that?

"You have been climbing the shrouds without them for the entire time aboard. I think your feet find the deck a better fit than your boots."

"I know not what coin we shall receive from Mr. Grogan. Do Americans use the same coin as the English and the Irish?"

Overhearing the question, an older seaman tells the young seamen, "Never fear, lads, the good folk of New Orleans find English coin as good as any provided by their citizens. Be careful they do not cheat you. A shilling is worth at least two American dollars. In some honest pubs, it will count as three. In truth, the ladies prefer English coins as they are honest silver, whereas American coins are less so."

Jamie, eager to learn more, asks, "What can we pay for a pint? And a good meal?"

The seaman smiles and replies, "Lad, if you pay more than tuppence for a pint, you are overcharged. A good meal may take three pence from your purse but surely no more."

Standing before Mr. Grogan, Jamie was surprised to learn his payment was one shilling and fifty pence. Knowing he was the most junior member of the crew, Liam was also happy to receive one shilling. Before they leave, Mr. Grogan looks at both boys sternly,

"Lads, you may go into New Orleans town. Be careful and watch each other's backs. There are many fancy women and bad fellows eager to take your coin. I expect you back on board before the eight bells watch ends. There will be no staying the night in New Orleans town."

The two boys follow crew members down the gangplank onto the dock and pause. Both realize they have no idea where they should go. Soon, they realize that other crew members are heading in a particular direction.

"What say we follow our shipmates?" said Liam.

"Let's hope they know where they are going.".

Following a group of four crew members, Liam and Jamie are awestruck by the number of shops, the diverse offerings within each, and the intricate carvings, jewelry, and clothing displayed by Africans. Jamie had only seen an African when the Primrose stopped in Liverpool. He reckoned more than half of the shops and artisans were African. Before they knew it, the group they were following had disappeared into a pub with a sign hanging over the entrance that announced this was the *Seaman's Rest*. The boys entered, surprised to see few in the pub beyond the crew members they followed. The three crew members motioned for them to join them at the table. One unfortunately was Turnbull, who smiled evilly at the two and said,

"What have we here, two young lads that cannot find their way without tagging along with their betters?"

The other crew members looked uncomfortable with Turnbull's comment but said nothing. A youngster of ten or so came to the table and asked what he could bring the group. Before anyone could respond, Turnbull tells the boy,

"Bring a pitcher of your best ale. These two lads, pointing to Liam and Jamie, shall pay for it in respect to their senior crew members."

With that, the other crew members smile at Liam and Jamie. Jamie and Liam look at each other in disbelief. Before the boy can leave, Liam takes his arm and asks, "\

"Who is the master of this inn?"

"Me father, Eric O'Malley, and I am Sean O'Malley, replies the boy.

"Let me help you with the ale, lad." Says Liam.

Liam follows the boy to an area just behind the bar. There, he finds a very large, and also red-headed Irishman. Liam looks at the man, "Sir, I am a poor boy from County Kilkenny, and the English sailors are trying to take the few coins we have. Since it is but me, my mate, Jamie, I fear we are no match for them."

Eric O'Malley looks at Jamie, smiles, and says,

"What might you be doing, sailing with a bunch of Englishmen? Are they shipmates?"

"They are Mr. O'Malley but no friends of ours, and the leader, Turnbull, takes every chance to torment the younger crew members."

At that, Sean, the boy, speaks up, "Father, the leader of the three, says we are to make the two lads pay for all the ale."

"Well, well, Englishmen taking poor Irishmen's wages. I think we shall find ways to remedy this. Sean, go to the quarters behind the inn and tell your uncles, Marcus and Theo, we may have to teach some Englishmen how to treat the Irish better."

Liam follows Mr. O'Malley and his son back to the tables in the inn. As Mr. O'Malley placed two large pitchers of ale on the table, he looked at the three older seamen. Recognizing the leader, Turnbull, he says.

"Englishman, I am told you want the two lads here to pay for your drink. For what reason do they suffer this take on their wages?"

Turnbull smirked and replied, "They are both sorry sailors and need to know how to treat their betters."

O'Malley stands to his full height, looks down on Turnbull, and asks, "Could it be that they are Irishmen?"

Turnbull, never fast to appreciate a potential problem, smirked again and said, "Irishmen make poor sailors and poor landsmen. We have no use for them at sea."

"I think you have mistaken my question for what it is not. I suggest, Englishman, that you look behind you. My two brothers and

I are always happy to let an Englishman know how we Irish feel about them."

Turnbull and his two shipmates turn and see two men even larger than O'Malley standing close behind them, realizing they are now in a poor position. Jones, of the two with Turnbull, makes a conciliatory effort, "Now, good sir, this was but a prank we were playing on the two lads." I believe there was some misunderstanding."

"Oh, shut your mouth, Jones," says Turnbull. "The lads deserve to know how things are aboard ship and ashore. We are the ranking sailors, and we deserve to receive our due rewards."

While this exchange occurs, the other two sailors with Turnbull fill their cups and quickly down what ale they can. Turnbull fills his cup as the other two stand and quickly make for the door. Turnbull is now alone at the table with Liam and Jamie and three very large Irishmen. He now realizes he is at a distinct disadvantage and unlikely to prevail, regardless of the circumstances. He quickly places fifty pence on the table and heads to the door.

"Thank you, Englishman, for your generous contribution to this Irish pub. We shall not forget you and hope never to have your face be seen again inside the door."

O'Malley turns to Jamie and Liam, "Well, lads, it looks like your shipmates have decided to try another inn. What say you two enjoy the ale that is paid for? We have some lovely mutton cook has prepared. I think the Englishman's coins will cover that, as well."

Liam and Jamie fill their cups and enjoy the ale provided by their departed shipmates. Plates of steaming mutton, potatoes, and greens are soon placed before them, and satisfied eating is the only sound heard. After two more cups of ale, Mr. O'Malley joins them at the table. He is curious about how two young Irishmen are on an English ship as crew. Having had no strong drink in many weeks, Jamie and Liam are as drunk as they have ever been.

In a halting yet coherent way, Jamie volunteers his story first. He was born in Cork City and immigrated to England with his parents when he was five. Finding no work after he turned thirteen, he joined a schooner crew out of Liverpool for a year and then worked on a fishing boat for a year before joining the crew of the Primrose two years ago. A little ashamed, Jamie confesses he never told Mr. Grogan he was born in Ireland, and because he sounded like another Liverpool lad, none of the crew assumed otherwise.

Now completely befuddled from the ale and no longer hesitant about who he is, Liam blurts out that his real name is Liam Flaherty. Jamie is taken aback and immediately asks why he uses another's name. Now only partially coherent, Liam tells the long story of how he and Michael Nolan participated in the demonstration against the Tithe Act in County Kilkenny. Sobbing, Liam recounts how Michael Nolan was apprehended, tried, and convicted of murdering a constable during the demonstration. Liam is sure Michael was hanged the day he left Liverpool on the Primrose. He explains to Jamie and Mr. O'Malley how he is a wanted man and would almost certainly suffer the same fate as Michael Nolan were he to fall into the hands of the Irish authorities. Finally, he describes his journey to Cork and eventually on the crew of the Primrose through the good graces of priests along the way. He looks at Jamie and says he could have never survived on the Primrose had it not been for Jamie.

Mr. O'Malley has learned of the bold effort in Carrickshock and now knows the full story from one of the participants there. His sympathy for Liam's plight prompts him to offer the two boys a bed for the night. Jamie is the first to remind Liam that Mr. Grogan required them to be back before the end of the eight bells watch. Jamie explains to Mr. O'Malley that this is midnight.

Liam is now in a quandary. He intended to jump ship as soon as it arrived in America. Now, it seems the time is right, mainly since he has contacted other Irishmen and can rely on their help. While he does not want to leave Jamie in a bad situation, he also realizes he may have no better opportunity. With the decision to remain in New Orleans, Liam and Mr. O'Malley go over some options for Jamie to explain how Liam left the ship and how Jamie can return without retribution from other shipmates.

Mr. O'Malley suggests the simplest of actions. First, Jamie finds other shipmates and tells the story about how he was kicked out of an Irish inn because he was an Englishman. Second, when Jamie returns to the Primrose, he tells Mr. Grogan that Liam/Michael was very drunk when Jamie was kicked out of the Irish inn. When Jamie returned to find Liam/Michael, no one knew where he was. A boy reported a young man was seen wandering about the docks and set upon by three bad-looking fellows. The boy knew not what became of the young man.

Jamie now realizes Liam/Michael had always intended to leave the ship once it reached America. He turns to Liam, "Why didn't you tell me, Michael? I know yours was a hard secret to keep. I shall miss you aboard the Primrose. It will be a long voyage back to Liverpool without you on the sails with me."

"I cannot thank you enough, Jamie, for your friendship and teaching. I would have never made it across the Atlantic without you. But you know now that I cannot return to Ireland or England."

"I do, Michael. It will be a sad voyage back to England without you. Putting up with Turnbull will be a task I do not relish. I expect Mr. Grogan will have to find someone to replace you. That said, I value our friendship and wish you well."

With a final toast of their cups, Jamie and Liam say farewell. Saddened, Jamie heads into New Orleans town to find his shipmates and tell the story they have constructed to explain Liam's disappearance.

Chapter 5: Finding His Way in America

Liam awakens the following day, hungover but light in spirit. He has made it to America and must now figure out what he will do for the rest of his life there. First things first, a hearty breakfast in the Inn helps with the hangover. As he eats with young Sean O'Malley, he wonders how Jamie fared with the story he was to give to Mr. Grogan.

Much earlier, the night before, Jamie and some of his shipmates returned to the Primrose before midnight. When inquiries were made about where Michael Nolan was, Jamie went to Mr. Grogan with the story he, Liam, and Mr. O'Malley had concocted. Unbeknownst to Jamie, Mr. Grogan had fully expected Liam to jump ship at the first port in America. He scowled for Jamie's benefit when he heard the story. He lamented that he would have to find a deckhand the next day and asked Jamie to inquire about Liam's whereabouts around the docks.

As Liam finished his breakfast, Jamie and another Primrose crew member walked the docks, asking if anyone had seen Liam. Again, one boy mentioned seeing a young man walking the docks late at night and being set upon by some poor-looking men. For the crewman, that was enough to stop searching and report to Mr. Grogan there was little chance of finding Liam. Two days later, the Primrose left for England with her holds full of cotton and a sad Jamie who would no longer have a friend aboard like Michael.

Liam knows the few coins he has left from Mr. Grogan will not go far. He must find work. He asks Mr. O'Malley where he might seek employment in New Orleans. Mr. O'Malley tells Liam so many Irish have immigrated to New Orleans that there is a surfeit of unskilled labor. If Liam had a trade, he would likely have many opportunities. Without a trade, most Irish immigrants leave New Orleans for the north, where prospects are better. Before they continue, Mr. O'Malley asks,

"Liam, can you read and write? Can you do numbers?"

"I can, Mr. O'Malley. I went through school, and me Mam was a very learned woman. She taught me after I finished school to do the higher numbers."

"Liam, you have some skills many of our countrymen who come to America do not." I think there may be a place for you here in New Orleans."

Mr. O'Malley knows that Mr. Leary, another Irishman who operates a shop selling boots, needs a clerk salesman. Without telling Liam, Mr. O'Malley goes to Mr. Leary's shop and tells Mr. Leary about Liam. After hearing Liam's story, Mr. Leary is willing to meet Liam to decide if he can do the job.

Later that day, Liam goes to New Orleans town to meet Mr. Leary. Mr. Leary is pleased Liam speaks well. He does a thorough job of testing Liam on his writing, but mainly on his mathematical abilities. Liam's performance convinces Mr. Leary he can do the job, and he is shortly offered the position. At the wonderous sum of ten dollars a month, Liam feels like he is a rich man. Working as a salesman in the boot shop is not difficult. Mr. Leary's boots are well known in New Orleans; many men and some women are repeat customers. Liam works hard to remember who the repeat customers are and makes an effort to greet them when they enter the shop. Mr. Leary appreciates Liam's efforts in this customer service and congratulates himself on hiring Liam.

Liam spends more time after closing the shop maintaining Mr. Leary's accounts. After two months, Mr. Leary has handed over the shop's books to Liam. He notes how quickly Liam alerts him when outstanding debts have exceeded a month. The weekly summary of receipts and expenditures he provides Mr. Leary is much more complete and accurate than Liam's predecessor. Within six months, Liam is a valuable member of the shop and the envy of the other two clerks. One of the other clerks, Mark Ketchum, a teenager like Liam, struggles to return the correct coin to customers. Liam recognizes that Mark's math skills are not as strong as they should be. After a few weeks of watching young Mark Ketchum struggle to add and subtract, Liam takes him aside and offers to help.

Mark Ketchum was born in New Orleans and got a job in Mr. Leary's shop because his father is one of Mr. Leary's best customers. A tall, thin boy of fifteen, Mark envies Liam's customer service and accounting skills. Mark's family has one of the most extensive plantations in the New Orleans area. Many of the slaves that work for

Mr. Ketchum receive their footwear from Mr. Leary. It is not unusual for Mr. Ketchum to order six or seven pairs of cheap boots or shoes in various sizes once or twice a month. When he comes in to order the shoes and boots for the slaves, he often orders two or more pairs of boots for himself. When Mr. Ketchum first came to the shop, Mark asked Liam to wait on him. Liam thought little of the request until he overheard Mr. Ketchum ask Mr. Leary if Mark was "working out."

Mr. Leary replied, "Mr. Ketchum, the boy is doing well, and I expect he will be as good as any clerk I have had within a few months."

"That is music to a father's ear," says Mr. Ketchum, "for I feared the lad was good for very little. He has no idea how much needs to be done around the plantation, and I cannot and will not tolerate idleness in anyone, son or slave."

Liam now understands why Mark wants him to wait for his father when Mr. Ketchum visits the store. Unfamiliar with how the large houses and plantations operate in and around New Orleans, Liam seeks more and more information from Mark Ketchum. Mark is grateful for Liam's help in improving his math skills and shares many stories with him of the big house and the cotton plantation that provides the basis for his family's fortune. Mark never wanted to attend the school his parents favored and confessed he learned little. Familiar only with subsistence farming typical in rural Ireland, Liam is amazed at the scope and the breadth of the cotton industry, and the Ketchums were among the leading suppliers in the New Orleans area.

He finds it difficult to imagine an enterprise with more than two thousand acres and hundreds of slaves tending and harvesting cotton.

Liam struggles to understand how dependent the cotton producers, like the Ketchams, are on slaves. He fully understands that for many Irishmen, their slavery is economic in a far different way than it is for slaves in America.

As Mark Ketchum educates Liam on New Orleans and cotton, Liam also learns from customers about America, his new home. Distances between towns Liam has only read about in books are now commonplace in southern America. The conversations he overhears about traveling by train to New York for a week are but one of many that Liam finds fascinating and piques his interest in learning more.

One woman customer, Mrs. Parmenter, fascinates Liam as she is well-dressed and polite to all. Liam imagines this is how a princess would act if he ever had the chance to meet a princess. When she visits the shop, she asks specifically for Liam and shares stories of her visits to Paris, New York, and Spain. Her visits to the shop are a bright spot in Liam's week. Toward the beginning of Liam's second year in Mr. Leary's shop, Mrs. Parmenter comes to the shop dressed all in black. She asks Liam for black boots that lace up to the calf. Before Liam can ask, Mrs. Parmenter quietly says,

"Young man, my husband has recently died. I am in mourning for the next three weeks and require an appropriate pair of boots to wear with my mourning clothes."

Liam's face immediately drops. "I am so sorry for your loss, Mrs. Parmenter. Please accept my condolences. I shall bring out some boots, I believe you will find appropriate."

"Thank you, Liam. My husband was a good man. Much older than I. He led a good, Christian life but died unexpectedly last Thursday. We fear it was something he ate, but the doctor is unsure. The funeral was held Sunday and attended by all who knew him."

What she does not indicate to Liam or anyone else is that it was a loveless marriage. The Williams, Lucy's parents, arranged the marriage when she was only sixteen to Nicholas Parmenter, a much older man, solely for the purpose of maintaining the business relationship between the two families. At sixteen, Lucy Williams Parmenter was unprepared for her marriage to the twice-widowed Parmenter. Immediately, she was treated as a decoration, an adornment that Parmenter showed off to all his friends whenever they held a party. Parmenter was not a cruel man but simply an icily reserved one who did nothing to help his teenage wife understand what her duties as the wife of a prominent businessman entailed. Their few intimate moments were difficult for Lucy, and she did her best to avoid them. She cannot help but be drawn to a young man years her junior.

She glances at Liam as he brings out two pairs of boots that he believes she will find suitable. Looking at both pairs, she turns to Liam,

"Is it possible for the heel and the sole on one to be put on a boot with the height and the loops like the other?"

"I will have to talk with Mr. Leary. He and the other bootmaker may be able to do as you ask, but I cannot say until I have talked with him."

"Please do so. I shall wait here until you return."

Liam quickly takes both pairs of boots to Mr. Leary and asks if what Mrs. Parmenter has asked can be done. Mr. Leary examines both boots and assures Liam that it can be done in three days. With that, Liam returns to Mrs. Parmenter.

"Mrs. Parmenter, Master Leary has assured me the boots you request will be ready in three days. Is that acceptable?"

"It is. You have my shoe form, so I need not return to have the boots fitted." Now seeking a chance to have more time with Liam, she asks,

"Will you deliver the boots once they are finished?"

"I shall, Mrs. Parmenter, and I thank you for your confidence in our work."

"Then I will see you at my home in three days with my new boots."

On the way back to her home, Lucy Parmenter works on a plan to seduce the young man who has drawn her fancy. She has never considered herself an evil person, but she has also never been one to accept limits on her own desires. Her marriage to Parmenter had been a barrier to much of what she desired. With Liam, she planned to take advantage of that freedom.

As Mrs. Parmenter left the shop, Mark Ketchum came to Liam's side,

"Liam, I do believe you have an admirer in Mrs. Parmenter."

"How can that be? I am but a poor clerk in a boot shop. I am certain she has many friends and admirers to choose from."

"That may be, but you don't see how she looks at you when you are fitting her boots. That is more than just an interest in the fit of a boot."

Liam dismisses Mark's suggestion, and three days later, Mr. Leary tells Liam Mrs. Parmenter's boots are ready for delivery. Liam carefully polishes the black boots and packs them in a box specially made for boots of that size. He checks the customer's books and finds Mrs. Parmenter lives more than five miles away on the banks of the Mississippi River. The home is listed in the books as Parmenter Hall. He asks Mr. Leary if he can take a carriage to deliver the boots. Mr. Leary agrees but cautions Liam to use the least expensive available.

Liam finds a small carriage called a trap that seats just one or two passengers behind the driver. He negotiates with the driver, who agrees to take Liam to the address for twenty-five cents, and the driver will remain for his return.

The five-mile trip to Mrs. Parmenter's is a wonder for Liam, who has seldom ventured far from New Orleans' town center. The closer they come to their destination, the grander and more opulent the homes. Liam had never seen buildings like this, even in books. Tall pillars grace every entrance, and the shine of the white stone reflects on the lush lawns and brightwork around the doors and windows. Parmenter Hall is easily spotted by the black drapery on the front door and windows, indicating a mourning period Liam recognizes. As he dismounts from the trap carriage, a grey-haired black man approaches him,

"Are you Master Liam with the boots for Mrs. Parmenter?"

"Yes, I am."

"I am Mrs. Parmenter's butler, Henry Pleasance. She is expecting you, please follow me to the tradesman's entrance."

As they walk down the pathway to the rear of the house, Liam finds himself gawking at its size and splendor. He cannot guess how many rooms there may be as he counts sixteen windows on the side he is walking along. Mr. Pleasance opens a door toward the back of the building, ushers Liam into a light-filled foyer,

"I shall tell Mrs. Parmenter that you are here. Please have a seat anywhere you like."

Liam looks around the foyer and sees ten chairs along the wall. Each is covered with fine silk. Fine paintings cover the walls, and polished wooden floors gleam in the early afternoon sun. This must be how the very rich live in America, thinks Liam. He recalls it was less than three short years ago he was hiding from the constables in a dirt dugout in the hills above Knocktopher; how things have changed.

"Master Liam, please follow me. Mrs. Parmenter will see you now."

Mr. Pleasance leads Liam along a long hallway to a room filled with light from floor-to-ceiling windows with their sides now draped in black. Seated at one end of the room, Lucy Parmenter closes the book she has been reading and motions for Liam to come forward. She smiles inwardly as she sees the young redheaded man stride toward her. Her thoughts of Liam over the past weeks have been strong and what many would consider improper for a woman of her station. She knows that any relationship with the young tradesman would be condemned from the start. The physical attraction she feels for him hardly conflicts with her sense of propriety. Her challenge is how to manage any affair that can be arranged.

"Liam, I am so glad you could fulfill my request for the boots. I look forward to trying them on. Henry, thank you for showing Mr. Flaherty in. I will call you when I need you."

Liam is flustered. He had never been in a room as elegant as this one. A crystal chandelier dominates the center of the room, and more than fifty candles will provide light after dark. Mirrors adorn multiple panels on the walls, and portraits of men in uniform cover one wall. He remembers why he is here and awkwardly carries the box of boots to the table in front of Mrs. Parmenter. As he places the box on the table, he looks at Mrs. Parmenter and suddenly realizes she is a beautiful woman, only a few years older than him. Disturbed that he has not noticed her youth before, he fumbles with the box and removes the boots individually. Lucy looks closely at Liam and recognizes he has entered a world entirely foreign. She feels a pang of sympathy for along with an increasing physical attraction to the young man. She has always lived in luxury in her family home and now in her husband's. What she did not expect was to notice how even more handsome a young man he was and how his physical presence awakened her sexuality. In doing so, she was reminded how long it had been since she had felt a man's arms around her. Shaking off the feelings momentarily, she looks approvingly at the boots.

"Liam, can we make certain that they fit?'

"Certainly, Mrs. Parmenter. May I remove the shoes you have on?"

Liam moves the table aside and drops to one knee in front of Lucy. He adroitly removes the slippers she is wearing and places them under the table. Then with the right boot, he lifts it so Lucy can examine it in detail.

"They look exactly as I specified. May I have them placed on my feet?"

Liam sees Mrs. Parmenter is wearing black stockings and wonders if those may compromise the fit of the boots. He holds the boot up,

"Will you be wearing the same stockings with these boots? I ask because the boots were made for light stockings, and if they are thicker, the fit may be tight."

"The stockings I wear are the ones I will wear with the boots, so let us have them on."

As Liam puts one foot into the boot and pulls the top of the boot up around her calf, Lucy Parmenter has a rush of warmth travel from her legs to her breasts. The feeling is so sudden that she blushes a bright red.

"Mrs. Parmenter, are you all right?" Did I cause you any harm in any way? If so, I beg your forgiveness, as it was unintentional on my part."

"Dear Liam, it has been so long since a man touched me, the feeling overcame me. Please come and sit by my side for a time."

Confused and not wanting to offend her, Liam joins Mrs. Parmenter on the sofa. Lucy can no longer hold her feelings in check and turns her face to his and softly asks,

"Liam, will you hold my hand for a little while? My husband was an old man who was cold and showed little affection. I crave the touch of a man, if for just a moment. I feel I have shriveled up like the flowers in winter. If I cannot feel love, at least some show of affection will supply."

Liam looks into the face of what he now recognizes as a beautiful woman whose youth and vibrant nature have been subdued for years. Unsure of himself, he holds out his hand and asks,

"What may I do to console you, Mrs. Parmenter? I have little experience with women and know little of how to respond to their needs."

"First, please call me Lucy. It is the name my family and I use. I would feel much closer to you if you were to call me Lucy."

With those words, Lucy pulls Liam's hand to her breast. As her emotions and longing for physical intimacy grow, she looks at Liam,

"Can you not feel my longing, Liam? I need a man's affection before I wither and die."

Liam is now reeling with his own emotions. Having only kissed a few girls in his life, to have a beautiful woman pull his hand to her breast and insist he show her affection is beyond his ability to respond immediately. Seeing his confusion, Lucy asks,

"Liam, have you ever been with a woman? I don't mean, have you kissed one? I mean, have you ever slept with a woman?"

"Mrs. Parmenter, Lucy. I have no experience with women and have never slept with a woman."

Seeing Liam's confusion, Lucy takes this as an opportunity to see how far Liam is willing to go.

"Let me assure you, my fine young man, that you are missing one of God's greatest gifts. The joy of two bodies coming together transcends the ordinary and makes the day brighter and the nights enjoyable."

She turns her head toward Liam, places her hand behind his head, and says, "Now kiss me and make me feel like a woman."

Liam is both confused and aroused and does as he is asked. This is beyond his comprehension. He does as she asks, taking her face in his hands, and kisses her cheeks before covering her mouth with shy, gentle kisses. Lucy is much more aggressive and pulls Liam's mouth wholly onto hers. Stroking his face, Lucy takes a deep breath and says,

"Are you prepared to take the next step, Liam? I want you to bed me, and I cannot wait much longer. I have longed for this far too long."

Liam's emotions swirl, and he is uncertain how to continue. He is confused and knows nothing good can come of doing anything with Lucy in her house.

"Lucy, you are still in mourning for your husband. I do not believe we should do anything more in this house. Is there somewhere we can meet?"

Lucy replies, "My family has a small cottage on the river just across from the entrance to Parmenter Hall. I walked there within the week, and there were no servants, just a caretaker who came by every other day or so. You can go there now, and I will meet you there within the hour. Look for a short path across from the entrance to Parmenter Hall. It is marked with lilacs and roses. The cottage is but a short distance from the path."

Liam looks into her glowing face and eagerly replies,

"I will meet you there."

"I will call for Henry and have him show you to the carriage. You and I shall be enjoying each other in a few hours."

Lucy has carefully arranged for the cottage to be empty and a trusted servant to ensure no one enters whenever Lucy is there.

Henry shows Liam to the door where his trap carriage waits. Liam bids Henry farewell and gets into the carriage. Liam's mind is whirling. He had never been so close to a woman. Now, this beautiful woman wants to take him to bed, and it is almost too much to comprehend.

As the carriage turns out of the gate from Parmenter Hall, Liam instructs the driver to look for a small path to the river framed by lilacs and roses. As the carriage makes its way, Liam spots the small pathway and stops the driver. Liam looks at the sun and then at the driver,

"Good driver. I'll be here for a few hours. If you return just after dark, I'll double your fare. Is that a bargain?"

"It is, sir. I shall return to this location just after dark and pick you up."

Chapter 6: The Affair

Liam walks down the path and sees the Mississippi River through the trees. He sees a small cottage nestled among the trees as he turns a corner. The river flows sluggishly along the bank, making small, wave-lapping sounds. Birds call to each other, and Liam thinks, "This must be as close to paradise as possible." He is excited and a little apprehensive about Lucy soon joining him in the cottage. Liam pulls open the door and sees a neatly arranged room that invites one to rest and relax. There is but one bedroom, and the bed seems large enough for two. Unsure of how to greet Lucy, Liam wanders around the cottage, waiting for her. He has no experience with women and has no idea what Lucy may propose.

Just as the afternoon light begins to filter through the window nearest to Liam, he hears a soft footfall outside and rushes to open the door. Lucy stands silhouetted in the doorway. Dressed in black with a veil, she appears to be anything but the woman who asked him to take her to bed. She slowly raises the veil and gives Liam a radiant smile that dispels any concerns her attire may have raised. She walks quickly to Liam, drops the black veil on a chair, and throws her arms around his neck. As she presses her body to his, she kisses him with a hunger Liam finds surprising and intoxicating.

"Take me now, Liam. I cannot wait a minute longer."

An hour later, exhausted, with Lucy's head deep into Liam's chest. Liam smells the honeysuckle in Lucy's hair and kisses her forehead. Lucy has opened up a whole new world of sensuality to Liam. He is as intoxicated with the experience as though he were heavy with drink.

"Lucy, I cannot get enough of you. You have captured me, and all I can think about is you. What am I to do?"

"We can do this as often as possible, but we must be discreet. Should anyone learn of this, it would cause me much harm. I will dress and leave before you. Please wait for an hour before leaving."

"How shall I know when we can meet again?

"I will send a message to you in your room in the boarding house. It will be a trusted servant who can bring you to me here."

Lucy dresses quickly and gives Liam a farewell kiss as she leaves. As she strides up the path to the entrance of Parmenter Hall, her thoughts are now on how to make this physical relationship with Liam last as long as possible. Aware that any whisper of the relationship with Liam would forever damage her standing in her social circle, she plans to keep it as circumspect as possible. A maid that Lucy has had since she was a child is both a trusted messenger and one that Lucy uses to keep the affair a secret.

After Lucy leaves, Liam leans back on the bed and reflects on the last hour. How is it I have met, fallen in love, and bedded the most beautiful woman I have ever known? If I must awaken from this dream, let it be much later in my life. As the shadows grow in the cottage, Liam realizes that the trap carriage will be waiting for him on the road above. He quickly dresses and begins the walk to the road. The trap is where he left it earlier, and the driver is eager to receive his extra coin. Liam returns to the boot shop to find it is closed. He walks to the boarding house, where he has a room, and falls into bed, ignoring the hunger pangs of a missed dinner.

Liam awakens before dawn the next day and, after a simple breakfast at the inn, opens the door of the boot shop and turns the sign, which shows OPEN. He has rehearsed the speech he will give Mr. Leary about why he did not return to the shop after delivering the boots to Mrs. Parmenter. A long walk back without the benefit of a carriage is one element of his failure to return, he tells Mr. Leary. The other is that, having returned to the town center of New Orleans, he was thirsty and stopped at an inn for a drink. The lack of food and drink made him ill, and he dared not put his illness on display at the shop. Mr. Leary accepted Liam's well-rehearsed excuse and thanked him for delivering the goods to a valued customer.

Over the following weeks, Liam and Lucy met at the cottage to revel in their physical relationship. Lucy never seemed to get enough physical intimacy from Liam, and Liam was more than ready to provide what he could. After the fifth week of their meetings at the cottage and Lucy's departure, Liam thought about the future. What could he offer Lucy? Is there a chance they could marry? If so, what would Liam bring to the union other than what Lucy had already experienced? These questions came more and more to mind during the days, and his work in the boot shop began to suffer as a result. Mr.

Leary quickly noticed his bright young clerk was no longer providing the work he had previously. Mr. Leary assumed Liam had found a girl, but Liam never mentioned anyone, and indeed, the other clerks were unaware of his outside activities. So, what was going on with Liam?

At the latest meeting in the cottage, when Liam and Lucy had dressed and she was about to leave, Liam asked, "Lucy, what is to become of us? It does not seem that we can keep this arrangement forever."

"Liam, just enjoy it while we can. Once my late husband's estate is settled, I will have more opportunities to spend time with you."

Lucy, do you know I have fallen deeply in love with you? I would do anything for you and wish to spend the rest of my life with you."

"Liam, I believe I know how you feel, and I have great affection for you. However, my future depends on settling my late husband's estate. Without that assurance, I have no future."

"Lucy, is a marriage in our future?"

Liam, I'm not able to answer that question at the moment. Perhaps in the future, it can be answered more definitively.

With those final words, Lucy hastens out the door, leaving Liam wondering what the future may mean for them and him alone.

Lucy has been carefully managing the meetings with Liam and realizes that the time has come to end the relationship. She has settled her former husband's estate and is now free to do what she wants with the rest of her life. To that end, she is increasingly available to the advances of unmarried men in her social circle.

For the next two weeks, Liam hears nothing from Lucy. Afraid to contact her at her home, he is miserable and heartbroken that something may have changed her mind about him. Plunging into his work on Mr. Leary's accounts, the days pass sluggishly for Liam. He avoids the other clerks who invite him to dinner with them. Alone in his room, Liam feels like the world is crashing down around his ears. Desolate, he imagines all the possible unfortunate things that can happen to Lucy. He is overjoyed when a message is left at his door the next day. He quickly opens the envelope to read the message contained therein:

Liam, I am no longer available to correspond with you. Please accept my sincere thanks for all your kind wishes. I leave for Europe in the morning with my fiancé, Mr. Oliver Grover. Enclosed is the payment for the boots, along with a token of appreciation for your additional effort.

Kind regards,

Mrs. Lucy Parmenter

Liam is devastated. He cannot believe Lucy has so casually cast him aside. At eighteen, his first physical relationship with a woman was unforgettable in his young life. He was convinced that he had found the love of his life. It was obviously not the case for Lucy. She engaged in the physical encounters as much as he did, but hers was just that, a physical, erotic relationship with no long-term expectation. Liam considers all the possible ways he might convince Lucy to stay and concludes nothing he can say or do will change the course of their relationship. The difference in their circumstances is now apparent. Liam never appreciated until now how different their social status was. Although she was willing to take the risks, she was also careful to ensure there was no long-term commitment. She has chosen someone else as her husband, and Liam is no longer part of her life. The next evening, in the Inn, while drinking the last of his ale, Liam realizes that his future is not in New Orleans and he must move on and seek his fortune elsewhere.

Over the following weeks, Liam will again be Mr. Leary's diligent clerk and bookkeeper. Mr. Leary sees the change in Liam and assumes he has had a teenage romance and is no longer enamored with a young lady. The almost two months of seeing a love-sick teenager contrast sharply with those of a broken-hearted young man.

On a sparkling Fall morning, a young man in a splendid officer's uniform enters the boot shop. As the senior clerk, Liam approaches and asks how he might be of service. The young officer smiles and says he is looking for boots to carry him on the marches his regiment conducts weekly. As Liam takes the officer's foot measurements, he asks,

"We have seen few Army in New Orleans. Are you now in the city?"

"No, my regiment is nearby, and I must find the best boot makers recommended by my Captain. We shall be looking to recruit soldiers for the regiment here in New Orleans. You will likely see one of my recruiters in the inn nearby. Many of those who wish to join the Army spend some time in the pub."

Liam reviews the various styles of boots that might meet the officer's requirements and wonders about life in the American Army. Curious, he asks the officer.

"And what might a young man joining your regiment expect? Where will he travel, and what experience will he gain?"

"Those are all good questions, my young fellow. I can tell you this. The Army will feed you, clothe you, and train you to be a member of a proud regiment. You will be paid a handsome wage and, depending upon your performance, will be promoted in due course to senior ranks. My regiment is the 4th Infantry Regiment, and it was one of the first raised during our War of Independence. It has served with distinction in all the conflicts the United States has had for the past fifty years. It is not a coincidence one of its more memorable actions was the British defeat here in New Orleans twenty years ago. President Jackson commanded the forces here in New Orleans and commended the regiment for its actions against the British."

The young officer opened a window to something Liam knew little about. For the next two weeks, he thought long and hard about what he might do in the future. With no prospects beyond New

Orleans, where could he go? Joining the Army seemed a reasonable opportunity. With that in mind, Liam saw a soldier in the pub talking with others. Striking in his blue and gold uniform, the soldier wears three stripes on his sleeve and a gold shoulder board. Taller than Liam, he has an air of solid dignity and can converse easily with the young men in the pub. When the soldier was alone, Liam approached and asked,

"May I join you? I met one of your officers in my shop and am curious what joining your regiment will mean. I am unfamiliar with the American Army, and I hope you can help."

The man looks at Liam as if sizing him up. Taking note of his Irish accent and red hair, he replies,

"Young Irishman, you will join many of your former countrymen in the finest regiment in the United States Army. It is a proud regiment and takes great pride in providing the highest level of training to each of its soldiers. We are visiting New Orleans to recruit suitable men for the regiment. Are you one of those suitable for the regiment?"

"I know not, sir, if I am suitable. I work in a boot shop as a clerk and accountant. I am looking to move beyond New Orleans. Is it possible for me to join the regiment?"

The soldier introduces himself as Sergeant Benjamin Pierce and tells Liam to come to their offices on the outskirts of New Orleans, where he may sign up as a regiment member. Armed with the information he sought, Liam must decide whether the Army is for him and how he will inform Mr. Leary that he has decided to leave his employment.

Saturday next is the end of the month, and Liam will bring the books to Mr. Leary to review the month's accounts. After he has provided Mr. Leary with all the accounts and satisfied any questions he asked, Liam puts the ledger books aside and asks,

"Mr. Leary, you have been a grand employer. I have learned a great deal from you and hope that my employment has been beneficial to you. I must now move beyond New Orleans. I shall work two weeks more to ensure young Mark Ketchum can manage the accounts. I hope you understand and approve my plan."

Mr. Leary, having observed Liam for the past two months, is not surprised by Liam's plan. He has no idea who the woman who stole Liam's heart is, but it is clear that she has broken it as well. He replies kindly to Liam,

"Lad, you have been a valuable clerk. You have done all that has been asked of you. For those reasons, I can but wish you well and Godspeed. Do you know where you're going?

"I have decided I am joining the Army. I have talked with one seeking men here in New Orleans, and I will soon be signing up to join the regiment."

The following two weeks pass quickly. Mark Ketchum has learned well from Liam and can master all the tasks Liam once performed. On his final day at the boot shop, Mr. Leary presents Liam with the finest boots the shop offers. Liam is overwhelmed by the generosity of the gift, which is equivalent to more than a month's salary for him. Sad that he will no longer be a member of the small shop community, Liam believes he has made a decision that will prove itself for the better. The other clerks wish him well as they shake his hand and slap him on the back.

Chapter 7: Joining the Army

Early the following day, Liam sets out to the address provided by Sergeant Pierce. He finds a nondescript building with two giant flags on either side of the entrance. One of the flags Liam recognizes as the American flag with its stars and red and white stripes. He does not recognize the other, for it is very ornate and has figures he does not recognize. Just inside the door, he sees an older man in a casual-looking uniform sitting at a rough desk. Liam approaches the desk, and the uniformed man looks up at him approvingly.

"Well now, young fella, are you looking to join the regiment?"

"I am, sir. An officer of this regiment has convinced me that the Army may have a place for me."

"You will not be calling me sir, young man. I am a corporal. We enlisted soldiers work for our living while officers go about telling us what to do. Before we have anything to do with you, we must know you are a healthy lad and carry no diseases. Give me your name and go sit on the bench with the other lads, and our surgeon will be with you shortly for an examination."

Liam gives the corporal his name, takes the seat as directed, and looks around the room behind the Corporal at the desk. What he sees is difficult for him to understand because the uniforms of those in the room all seem different. He recognizes the officer whom he spoke to earlier in the week. A much older man in a uniform, somewhat like the young officer's, seems to be doing all the talking. He has more braid on his uniform and a very impressive mustache. Around the room are other soldiers in odd pieces of uniform. A tall, thin man with almost no hair on his head sports three gold chevrons below a gold diamond. When he speaks, both officers and the other soldiers listen closely to what he says. The Corporal at the desk then motions to Liam to come closer.

"I see you're watching the officers behind me. The tall man is First Sergeant Harkins. He is the senior enlisted man in the regiment. It would be best to steer around him until you finish your training. He has a dislike for civilians and amateur soldiers."

Just then, a man in a white coat comes out of a door near the bench and motions for the nearest man to come with him. The remaining two soldiers, with Liam being the last of the two, slide down toward the door that just closed. Fifteen minutes pass until the first man exits the door, followed by the man in the white coat. The young man then follows the man in the white coat to the corporal at the desk.

"Corporal Scoggins, this man is fit and can be recruited into the regiment."

"Aye, Surgeon Tompkins." Corporal Scoggins makes a mark in his ledger. "I will send him on to the adjutant."

Surgeon Tompkins motions for the next man to follow him into the examining room. Five minutes later, the surgeon slaps open the door and pulls the man to Corporal Scoggins's desk.

"What idiot recruited this poor man? He has no teeth and is nearly fifty years of age!"

"Pardon me, Surgeon Tompkins, but I know not which party is to blame. We have had so many come to this recruitment, I cannot tell who did the recruitment."

Surgeon Tompkins turns to the man whom he has just rejected. "My good fellow, you shall not join this regiment. I wish you well. Please see yourself out."

Corporal Scoggins makes a line through an entry in his ledger and points to the door.

Surgeon Tompkins motions for Liam to join him in the examination room.

"How old are you, young man?"

"I am 18 years of age, sir," replies Liam.

"Take off your shirt and open your mouth."

For the next ten minutes, the surgeon examines Liam's teeth, checks his arms and legs for damage, and listens closely to his chest with something that, to Liam, looks like a hearing horn. He directs Liam to put his shirt back on and follow him. As they leave the examination room, the surgeon leads Liam to the corporal's desk.

"Corporal, if we could recruit more young men like this, the regiment would be far better than the poor lot we have seen most recently. Send this young man off to the adjutant."

Corporal Scoggins makes a mark in his ledger and directs Liam to an office across the entry hall. On the door, Liam reads, "Adjutant of the Regiment" written crudely above the handle. He knocks gently on the door. A loud "Enter" answers his knock.

Liam opens the door and finds a large, overweight man sitting behind a large table. The man's face is flushed, and his uniform seems strained at every button and seam. The man looks Liam up and down and motions him to the table.

"Lad, can you read? If not, I can read for you."

"I can read."

"You will read that your enlistment in the regiment is a contract. It is a contract you break at your own risk. It is on the table here, and I suggest you read it now and sign it. Once you have signed the contract, you will gather your belongings and report back at first light tomorrow. From here, you will be transported to the regimental training camp some distance from town.

Liam fills in his name and birth date and reads the contract. He is surprised to note that his monthly pay is a measly $6, compared with the $10 he was paid each month at the boot shop. Not surprised by the penalty for desertion, he is alarmed by the penalties for insubordination, loss of military equipment, and failure to muster on time. He signs the contract, hands it back to the Adjutant, and asks, "What is required of me, now?"

The adjutant examines the neat signature and places the contract on the stack nearest to him. Turning to Liam, he responds,

"Lad, this is your last night as a civilian. Report here at first light tomorrow morning. Should you fail to report, you will have breached your contract, and I shall have the police find you."

Smarting a little from the intended rebuke, he returned to his room in the boarding house. He began to gather his clothing and the few personal items he had collected. He was particularly careful of the new boots he received from Mr. Leary. His thoughts on what boots the Army may provide him were secondary to his curiosity about the training. Little did he know it would be a significant change in his life.

Early the following day, after a quick bite of breakfast, Liam arrives at the recruiting office of the 4th Infantry Regiment. Twenty men are milling around, waiting for the same transportation that the Adjutant promised Liam. As the day brightens with full sun, two wagons pull into the area in front of the recruiting office, accompanied by a thin, uniformed man with two gold stripes on his sleeve, riding a gelding he controls with some difficulty.

The thin man calls out to the crowd, "At ease. Pay attention to my instructions. Each wagon can carry as many as twelve men. Divide yourselves into two groups and get in the wagons. Do not dally."

As he is closest to the wagon, Liam quickly climbs aboard, joined by eight other men. Liam looks at his travel companions and is surprised that some appear no older than sixteen, if that is the case.

Few of the men are much older than Liam. Some bigger in frame, but most of an average build and no taller than he.

Liam turns to the one sitting closest to him, "My name is Liam Flaherty. What might yours be?"

"My name is Michael Banyon. I see you are Irish. My family arrived in America early, and I was born in New Orleans. When did you come to America?

Three years ago, I worked in a boot shop before signing up to join the Army. Do you know anything about the training camp and what might be planned for us?"

Before Michael could answer, an older man of almost twenty looked at them and exclaimed,

"You shall learn to march and march and march some more. When you are tired of marching, you will be forced to march more. Once you have received your musket, you will be taught how to load, fire, and reload. After that, you will march some more. My brother enlisted last year and told me all about the Regimental training. I see it as a necessary evil."

After traveling for half the morning, the wagon comes to a halt. The thin horseman shouts, "Dismount and line up with the tallest man to the right and the shortest to the left."

The twenty scramble out of the wagons and awkwardly attempt to line up by height. After switching back and forth, Liam finds himself in the middle of a line of twenty, neither the tallest nor the shortest.

The thin man dismounts from his horse, approaches the line of twenty, and commands, "Count off by two from the tallest man." A series of blank looks from the twenty causes the thin man to walk to the tallest in the line, poke him in the chest, and shout, "You are number one." He then goes to the next man in line and shouts, "You are number two. Now, do you ignorant bunch of bastards understand?"

With that last shout, the men count off by two. The thin man then shouts, "All number twos, step back and form a second line behind the first. Once you have done that, turn to your right and try to follow me in some semblance of order."

The two columns march out of step, with the thin man leading his horse and the two columns. The thin man calls for the columns to halt and, pointing with his right arm to a square hut, shouts,

"This is the quartermaster's. Here, you will be provided with a uniform. The uniform is for your training and will be replaced with a proper regimental one if and when you complete the first three weeks of training. Liam's group of ten moves into the hut and finds mounds of clothing overseen by two older men. As each recruit enters the hut, the first man looks him up and down and shouts a size to the second man. The second man then rummages through the pile of clothes and retrieves a shirt and a pair of pants. Liam soon finds himself with a white shirt and a pair of pants that were thought to be medium. The thin man directs the group, now clutching their new "uniforms," to a line of tents. In each tent are four rough cots made of wood. Ropes across the sides hold threadbare mattresses. Liam finds himself in a tent with three others, each looking as bewildered as he is. Once all twenty recruits are assigned a tent, the thin man shouts,

"Off with your civvy clothes, put on your uniforms, and stand in front of your tent."

The twenty scramble out of their clothes and put on the blue pants and white collared shirts issued by the quartermaster. Soon, all twenty recruits are standing in front of their tents in some semblance of uniformity. Liam sees that some younger recruits have poorly made boots, while others have very thin shoes that have seen much wear. He is even more grateful to Mr. Leary for his fine boots. The thin man directs the twenty to form into a four-abreast and five-deep formation. Each tent will form a line, with the tent group behind it positioned behind another. Liam's tent group is closest to the thin man, so he becomes the first line, and the other four tent groups arrange themselves behind them. The thin man ignores their clumsy effort to form the ranks and strides to the front of the formation.

"I am Corporal Jenkins. For the next weeks, I shall be your drill instructor. When called to formation, you will do so in the order you are in now. I expect you to do so quickly. Now, the first order you will receive is 'Attention.' I am standing at attention. My heels are together, my feet pointed slightly outward, and my thumbs close to the sides of my trousers."

Loudly, Corporal Jenkins shouts, "Attention."

The twenty recruits in formation attempt to stand as directed by Corporal Jenkins. The Corporal then walks along each file and corrects half of the formation's posture, foot alignment, and arms. Jenkins then moves again to the front of the formation.

"The next command you will receive is 'At ease.' My legs move to the width of my shoulders, and my arms are crossed behind my back with my right hand flat on my left hand. At no time does your head move left or right. I shall now give you the commands until you understand what to do."

For what seems to Liam like an hour, Corporal Jenkins repeatedly commands "Attention" and "At ease." The recruits snap to attention more precisely each time and quickly assume the at-ease position. Jenkins identifies one or two recruits who are slow to respond or whose positions need correction. While at ease, Corporal Jenkins walks off behind the formation. He returns quickly, following an officer resplendent in the formal regimental uniform. Jenkins quickly commands, "Attention," as the pair moves to the front of the formation. The officer looks slowly over the formation and nods to Jenkins. Jenkins then commands, "At ease."

The officer folds his arms behind his back, walks to the left side of the formation, and, speaking loudly, says.

Chapter 8: Regimental Training Camp

"I am Captain Gardiner. I am the Commanding Officer of 2nd Company, 4th Infantry Regiment. If you finish your training satisfactorily, you will join the Company and become a member of the regiment. I trust Corporal Jenkins will provide all the training you require. He and I will decide if you can join the regiment. You should address your concerns and needs to Corporal Jenkins until you become a regiment member. Until then, I wish you good luck. Listen well to Corporal Jenkins, and you will succeed."

Before he can turn away, Corporal Jenkins commands, "Attention," and salutes Captain Gardiner smartly. Turning back to the formation, he commands, "At ease."

The late summer sun is now high in the sky, and all the recruits are hot and tired. Liam is thirsty and raises his hand to get Corporal Jenkins' attention. "Corporal, is there water we may have?"

"Aye, lad, there is water in the feeding tent. You will be marched there in due course. Once you have been issued your canteens, you will be expected to keep them filled and drink whenever possible. Until then, you will learn how to march properly."

For the next hour, Corporal Jenkins instructs the recruits to step off with their left foot and maintain their pace at the cadence he calls out. The formation marches forward and backward across the field until one of the recruits falls forward onto his face. Corporal Jenkins pulls a round canteen from his belt and pours it over the fallen recruit's head, and when he revives, he gives him a small drink. When the young man regains his feet, the formation marches forward to a larger tent group from which cooking smells tantalize the hungry and thirsty recruits.

Liam and his tent mates move through a line, are handed metal pans and cups, and have the pans filled with meat and potatoes, while the cups are filled with coffee. An open wooden keg of water soon finds the recruits emptying their coffee cups and refilling them with water. Liam finds the meat and potatoes filling and the water cool and refreshing. Corporal Jenkins directs the group into formation within minutes of the last recruit's meal.

"Recruits, your drill and marching must be mastered before you take up your musket. Each soldier must act as part of one company. We rely on the company to be able to participate in the regiment when called upon. When you are all able to act as one, we shall then take up the muskets and begin training you as soldiers."

For the rest of the afternoon, the twenty recruits march shoulder to shoulder, learn flank movements, and maintain a tight formation. Liam is surprised at how easily he can follow the Corporal's orders without thinking. By late afternoon, it is apparent that the recruits are exhausted. After one last turnaround in what has become their drill field, the recruits are dismissed until dinner. Liam and his three tent mates drop onto their rough cots. No words are spoken, for all can hear exhaustion emanating from each cot.

Corporal Jenkins shouted to the tents in what seemed but a few minutes, "Fall in." The recruits scramble from their cots and assemble in their now familiar formation. Corporal Jenkins marches the formation to the cooking tents, and the process of being fed at lunch is repeated for dinner. Liam sits with his tent mates and turns to the other three.

"My name is Liam Flaherty. What might your name be?"

The youngest of the four replies, "My name is John Morrissey."

The third member speaks up, "I am Jonathon Pruitt."

The three look at the fourth member, expecting him to reply. Instead, he looks at the three and says nothing. His expression is one that some might consider fear.

Liam looks straight at the fourth member of the tent group, "What shall we call you?"

"T, t, t, Tucker," is the only reply. Liam recognizes that his inability to speak clearly or stutter is why he did not speak up.

"Well, Tucker, we are glad to share our tent with you and shall look forward to becoming members of the regiment."

With those warm words from Liam, the other two tent mates clap Tucker on the back and give him small words of encouragement. "We must work together," says Pruitt. Morrissey follows with, "Never fear, Tucker. We are all in this together."

Corporal Jenkins marches the recruits back to their tents and directs them to clean up and be ready for the reveille call at first light. The four tent mates quickly wash up at the communal wash tub and wear their civilian clothes to sleep in. Each, now almost overcome with exhaustion, falls asleep.

An unfamiliar yet demanding bugle call awakens Liam. The bugle call was so loud that it seemed the bugler was at his tent. The four scramble quickly into their uniforms and form up in front of their tent. Corporal Jenkins gives the command, "Fall in," and the twenty quickly make their formation. Breakfast formation is a repeat of the previous day's lunch and dinner. Liam is pleased there is meat, potatoes, bread, and coffee. Being well-fed for breakfast promises a full day of drill and marching. Immediately after breakfast, the group returns to the Quartermaster's tent, where they are issued boots.

Having worked in Mr. Leary's boot shop for two years, Liam knows well-made and less well-made boots. In his opinion, the boots he is issued are somewhere between well-made and not-so-well-made boots. He is satisfied they will do, but plans to wear his own whenever possible.

The twenty recruits in new boots removed grass on the drill field for the next four days. Some recruits' boots are not well fitted, and they suffer the consequences of blisters and sore feet. Liam and his three tent mates are fortunate, and by the fourth day, their boots are well broken in and more comfortable. Before being marched to dinner on the fourth day, Corporal Jenkins gives each recruit a wooden facsimile of a musket. When each recruit has received his wooden "musket," Jenkins explains,

"For the next days of your training, you will learn how to shoulder your musket, present your musket, and move forward with your musket. Only after you have mastered these will we begin the marksmanship you will learn with the musket."

Two days later, after many drill movements with their wooden "muskets," Corporal Jenkins marches the recruits to a large building beyond the woods lining the drill field. The recruits have returned their wooden "musket" to another quartermaster and will soon receive their real muskets. A small man of leathered features stands at the door of the building. After telling the formation to stand at ease, he introduces himself,

"I am Sergeant Killner, the regimental armorer. I am responsible for the weapons of the regiment. I am to issue each of you a musket. The 1816 musket is the standard for the regiment. It is a fine weapon and will perform well if you take care to maintain it as you should. Now, form a line to the right of the doorway. When I hand you a musket, you must read off the number above the flintlock as he points to the side of the musket he is holding. I will write that number in the ledger, and you will sign your name or make your mark beneath the number. Do you understand?"

In unison, the recruits respond, "Yes, Sergeant."

The next hour is spent with Sergeant Killner issuing muskets, the recruits signing for each, and each recruit receiving a cartridge pouch embellished with the regimental crest on the leather. Few recruits have ever handled a real musket, and their curiosity is apparent. As soon as the first recruit receives his musket, Corporal Jenkins directs him to stand at ease with the musket at his right side and his right hand along the muzzle. To the line waiting to receive their muskets, he points to the recruit now standing with his musket and says,

"Once you have your musket, form and stand as this recruit stands with his musket."

Once the last recruit has been issued his musket and joined the formation, Corporal Jenkins commands "Right shoulder arms" and "Forward march." After hours of practice with their wooden "muskets," placing their real muskets on their right shoulders is quickly accomplished. Jenkins marches them a mile down a dusty road to what the recruits soon learn is their shooting range. Few realize how many hours will be spent at this lonely site, perfecting two critical skills: loading and firing their muskets.

The recruits are directed to stand at ease while Corporal Jenkins lifts the musket he has been carrying. As he holds the musket, he begins,

"This musket fires a sixty-nine-caliber ball. It does so by firing the gunpowder placed in the barrel, followed by the ball. Each of you open your cartridge pouch and pull out one of the cartridge sleeves.

Follow my steps as I load the weapon. First, tear open the cartridge sleeve with your teeth, careful not to spill any powder. Next, pull back the lock, the lever closest to your thumb. This will open the pan, where you will place a small pinch of powder from the cartridge sleeve. Now close the lock and pan. Next, pour the powder into the muzzle. Finally, take the ball from the cartridge sleeve with the paper cartridge and place it in the muzzle of the musket. To seat the ball and the powder, pull your ramrod from under the barrel, place it in the muzzle, and push firmly to seat the ball. Your musket is now loaded and ready to be fired."

Liam has no difficulty following Corporal Jenkin's instructions and quickly primes and loads his musket. Two of his tent mates are also following the instructions. Tucker, however, seems unable to understand the loading sequence and has dropped the powder and ball into the muzzle without priming the pan. Jenkins sees this and quickly grabs Tucker's musket.

"Are you daft, boy? How will you fire your musket if the pan is not filled with some powder?"

With that, Jenkins lifts Tucker's musket to his shoulder, pulls back the lock, and pulls the trigger. Nothing happens. He then shoulders his musket, pulls back the lock, and pulls the trigger. The resounding blast from the musket causes Tucker and the other recruits to jump.

"Now, daft boy, take another cartridge, tip some powder in your pan, and fire your musket into the air as I did."

Clumsily, Tucker takes a paper cartridge and tears it open with his teeth. As he places some powder in the pan of his musket, Liam sees Tucker has spilled gunpowder on his lips and chin. Before Liam can say or do anything, Tucker raises his musket to his shoulder and pulls the trigger. The gunpowder in the flash pan fires the musket and ignites the gunpowder Tucker has spilled on his lips and chin.

Tucker drops his musket, grabs his face, and screams, "I am burned and blinded."

Bemused, Corporal Jenkins looks at Tucker and the rest of the recruits, "It seems like Daft Boy here has demonstrated how not to load your musket. Calm down, boy. The little burn on your face might improve your appearance, but it will surely help you remember how to load your musket properly."

Each recruit loads and fires his musket five times in the air for the next hour. Liam sees that his cartridge pouch has only five paper cartridges remaining and wonders what is next. Corporal Jenkins quickly provides an answer by pointing out a series of small tree stumps arranged about twenty-five yards from them.

"Here are five targets for each of you to shoot at this afternoon. I will determine if any can meet the regimental standard of firing three shots in a minute. You four," pointing to Liam and his tent mates, line up along this line, and when I give the commands, you will load and fire as quickly as you can."

Liam, Tucker, Morrisey, and Pruitt line up on the line Jenkins has scratched into the dust. They stand with their muskets on their right shoulders. Jenkins commands, "Present arms, load, and prepare to fire."

The three quickly load their muskets and place them across their chests. Tucker drops his first paper cartridge, frantically grabs another from his cartridge pouch, and eventually loads his musket. Jenkins frowns at the delay caused by Tucker and gives the following two commands, "Ready, aim fire."

Three muskets fire. Tucker's misfires because he has not put enough gunpowder in the pan. Jenkins, now red-faced and angry at Tucker, pulls him aside. Liam and the other two are busy reloading and do not see Jenkins repeatedly striking Tucker with his fist. Jenkins watches the three and checks his timepiece. The minute is up, and the three have only managed to fire twice. None of the tree stumps has suffered any damage, although a few furrows in the dust indicate close shots.

The remaining four groups do no better than Liam's, and after the final group of four has had their minute to fire, Jenkins calls for all five groups to check and ground their weapons. He gives his timepiece to Liam to mark the time and tells the recruits, "This is what is expected of you in the regiment." Jenkins places the stock of his musket on the ground and quickly loads and fires. When Liam calls "Time," Jenkins has loaded and fired his musket four times. The recruits also found each of the four stumps had some bark taken from it by Corporal Jenkins's fire.

"Now, recruits, if you can load and fire thrice a minute, you might make a soldier in the regiment. If not, I believe another line of work is better suited to you."

Corporal Jenkins repeatedly leads the recruits through dry fire exercises for two hours. As the recruits begin to adapt to the sequence of pulling the cartridge, priming the pan, dropping the powder and then the ball into the barrel, ramming it home, and finally returning the ramrod to its holder, it is apparent a few more recruits cannot perform. After the hours of practice, Jenkins calls out the poor-performing recruits and dismisses the others to their tents. In doing so, he calls Liam,

"Recruit Flaherty, march the recruits back to the tents."

Liam is taken aback by this sudden requirement to be in charge. Hesitantly, he says, "Fall in." The other recruits respond as they have been taught. Liam gives the command, "Right face, forward march." He halts the formation when they arrive at their tents and dismisses them to their tents. To himself, Liam wonders if he has found his calling. On return to the tent, his two remaining tentmates soon burst his enthusiasm by ridiculing his performance in the drill.

Chapter 9: The Real Army

After six weeks in the training encampment, Liam has learned the fundamentals of marksmanship, drill, and ceremonies. As a Private in the 4th Infantry Regiment, he wears his dress regimental uniform and his working uniform. His musket is always close by, and his ability to load and fire three times within a minute now seems automatic.

What is unexpected and not well received are all the other "duties" privates in the regiment must perform. From assisting in the soldier's kitchen to maintaining and repairing the regimental wagons and caring for the regimental horses, he seldom has time for much else. The daily formations and drills are now the tempo of his life.

Assigned to the second company of the regiment, Liam seldom sees the company commander. Captain Gardiner, but First Sergeant Harkins seems to be everywhere. Corporal Jenkins, now Liam's squad leader and promoted to Sergeant, keeps a close eye on the new members of the regiment. Over the succeeding seven months, Jenkins notes that Liam is quicker than his comrades, efficiently manages the few administrative tasks assigned to him, and has the respect of both the older soldiers and the new soldiers.

After morning formation, First Sergeant Harkins calls Sergeant Jenkins to his office and asks if any new soldiers might be useful as a company clerk. Jenkins immediately thinks of Flaherty and recommends to the First Sergeant that he interview Liam. First

Sergeant Harkins agrees to speak with Liam and directs Jenkins to send him to the office after evening formation.

Sergeant Jenkins calls Liam aside after lunch and tells him to report to the First Sergeant after the evening formation. Being called to the First Sergeant is seldom a good thing, and Liam's response is hesitant.

"Sergeant Jenkins, is this a bad sign? I never heard a report to the First Sergeant to be anything but bad news."

"Flaherty," responds Jenkins. "No, lad. This is a good omen. The First Sergeant is looking for a clerk, and I have recommended he see if you can fill the bill."

"I have no idea what a company clerk might do, Sergeant Jenkins. How should I be able to do the job?"

"Make sure your uniform is as good as can be, answer the First Sergeant's questions truthfully, and you should have no issues. A clerk is little more than an errand boy for the First Sergeant, so do not fancy yourself becoming more than that."

Liam prepares his uniform and shines his boots for the remainder of the afternoon. When he stands in the evening formation, his appearance is the best he can make it. With some trepidation, he proceeds to the headquarters building and the First Sergeant's office. At the door of the office, Liam knocks. A gruff "Enter" responds to his knock.

Liam enters the office to find First Sergeant Harkins sitting behind a field desk with papers scattered over the top and some even on the floor. Harkins is all angles—square head, jutting jawline, straight shoulders, and long, narrow fingers. Even the short, grey haircut seems to have been cut square on his head. Liam stops at the desk and reports,

"Private Flaherty reporting as ordered."

"Stand at ease, Flaherty."

"Can you read and write, Flaherty?"

"Yes, First Sergeant, I can read, write, and do the numbers."

"Let's see how good you are. Pick up the papers on the floor, read them to me, and if there are numbers to add, do so."

Liam gathers a sheaf of papers on the floor next to the desk. He places them in an orderly stack and looks at the first one. He recognizes the first paper as some inventory with lines of items and columns of figures. Glancing over the entire sheet, he begins to read,

"Requisition of supplies to support the second company for the dates October 1834 through December 1834. Line one, cartridges, musket, .60 caliber, 1000. Line two, muskets, Model 1916, 10. Line three, kitchen mess equipment, 3."

"That is enough of that page. Read the next," barks Harkins.

Liam flips to the next page and begins, "Morning Report, Second company, 4th Infantry Regiment, for October 1, 1834. Officers 4,

Sergeants 10, Corporals 15, Private soldiers 118. Submitted this date, Gardiner, Captain, Commanding, Second Company, 4th Infantry Regiment."

"Now, read the first page, add the figures on each line, and place the totals where they belong," says Harkins as he hands Liam a ledger.

Liam scans the page and notes that each line represents a specific item of equipment, and the column to be added is the total for that item. Having maintained Mr. Leary's books for over a year, Liam has no trouble adding the column and placing a number total at the bottom of the page. Handing the ledger back to First Sergeant Harkins, Liam asks, "Is there any more, First Sergeant?"

"Flaherty, you have passed my test. I expect you here immediately after the first formation tomorrow morning. You should wear your work uniform. Tell Sergeant Jenkins I will see him in my office tomorrow after breakfast."

"Yes, First Sergeant," replies Liam as he about-faces and leaves the First Sergeant's office.

Still dazed by the events in the First Sergeant's office, Liam sees Sergeant Jenkins across the drill field and walks quickly to him. "Sergeant Jenkins, do you have a minute?"

"Has the First Sergeant thrown you from his office, Flaherty?"

"No, Sergeant. He told me to report after the first formation tomorrow. I guess I will work for him as a clerk because he said I passed his test. He also asked you to come to his office after breakfast."

"Well, Flaherty. It looks as though you have good news, and I have news that will be less so."

"How is that, Sergeant?"

"Come, lad. You are to be the First Sergeant's clerk, and I have lost another good soldier to the First Sergeant. That is your good news, and mine is less so. Good luck, and I shall see you in the First Sergeant's office tomorrow."

That night, Liam wonders what his new job will be and how it will affect his time in the Army. He has seen a clerk or two about the company but never paid much attention to them. They always seemed in a hurry, scurrying about and carrying papers. As he falls asleep, he has a nightmare in which he carries more and more papers, dropping them everywhere, and never finds the ones he has dropped.

After first formation and a quick breakfast, Liam goes quickly to the First Sergeant's office. Knocking again on the frame of the now open door, First Sergeant Harkins gruff, "Enter," greets Liam. There are now more papers on Adam's desk and the floor.

"Flaherty, get busy picking up these papers and sorting them out. Put the morning reports in one pile, requisitions in another, and anything else in a separate pile. You will organize them once they are collected. I have letters to write and need the desk cleared."

Following the First Sergeant's orders, Liam gathers papers on Harkins' desk and the floor. Once the three piles are made, Liam begins their organization. First, he places the oldest documents at the bottom of each pile so the most current document is on top. The task is straightforward for the morning reports, and most dates are first and foremost. Requisitions are less so as the dates are not always in the same place or even readable in some cases. The miscellaneous pile is much more challenging. Liam finds letters from other regiments, Army departments, and individuals that Liam does not recognize among the many pieces of paper in that pile. Liam tries sorting them by recipients or dates and finds it almost impossible, as many are difficult to categorize. Finally, he has multiple piles of papers he can readily identify.

Looking up from the floor where he has organized the papers, Liam sees First Sergeant Harkins writing furiously at his desk. Waiting for Harkins to pause, Liam assumes the papers should be kept separately. Wanting to demonstrate initiative, he looks around the office for some containers that might work to hold everything. Seeing the cartridge boxes stacked alongside the wall, Liam quickly relocates cartridges from half-filled boxes, leaving him with two boxes that he can divide into four separate sections. What Liam does not know is First Sergeant Harkins is watching closely. Just as Liam finishes putting the papers in each container, Harkins rises from his desk and asks,

"Just how are we to find the papers we need, Flaherty? I see no organization."

"I will mark each container with the papers in it and organize them according to date, with the newest at the top," replies Liam.

From that moment on, and for the next four months, First Sergeant Harkins relied on Liam more and more to maintain the mounds of paper that seemed to accumulate in the First Sergeant's office. Following morning formation, Liam would run to each squad area and receive detailed reports on the soldiers assigned. With the information, Liam began compiling the morning report. This critical document listed the number of soldiers present for duty and the number who might be away, sick, or otherwise unavailable for duty.

Although the Company Commander, Captain Gardiner, signs the Morning Report, the First Sergeant must put it together. First Sergeant Harkins now relies on Liam to assemble the information and put it in the prescribed format. After a month, Harkins gives Liam's work only a cursory review before taking it to Captain Gardiner. The Regimental Adjutant receives the company's Morning Reports and is pleased to note that the Second Company's reports are now much better than before and advises Captain Gardiner to "keep up the good work." Gardiner is well aware that First Sergeant Harkins has taken Liam on as his company clerk. When they are out of earshot of soldiers, Gardiner compliments Harkins on his selection of Liam.

A benefit of working in the Company Orderly Room is that one often overhears plans and decisions long before they are communicated to the regular soldiers. After four months with the First Sergeant, Liam overhears the likelihood that the Regiment will relocate. Liam hopes to move north, as he is still uncomfortable in Louisiana's heat and humidity. Soon enough, he learns that the Regiment will be moving to a Fort named Brooke somewhere to the east. When and how the Regiment will travel there is yet to be announced.

Chapter 10: On to Florida

In the heat of a July morning, the first elements of the 4th Infantry Regiment boarded the steamship Orleans. Captain Gardiner, First Sergeant Harkins, and company clerk Liam Flaherty were among the lead group. Liam watched in wonder as the large paddle wheel at the stern of the ship began slowly turning. As the paddle wheel speed increased, so did the ship's speed. Liam squinted into the rising sun and wondered how far they would go and where this Fort Brooke might be. Although Liam knows the regiment has been stationed at Fort Brooke for two years, he has never been told where it is located in the area called Florida. Some have mentioned that the locals are not friendly. Liam has no experience with the indigenous people and wonders what they may be like.

By evening, the dark smudge on the horizon to their left gave way to a taller smudge of land ahead. Liam joined his former recruit tentmates Morrisey and Pruitt at the rail in the ship's bow. Jostling between the two, Liam asked if either of the other two knew where Fort Brooke was located. Pruitt said he had heard it was on the coast of Florida. As they watched, the steamship entered a bay and headed toward a dock at what looked to be the head of the bay. The dock was barely large enough to let the Orleans come alongside and put out two gangplanks. Soon, two columns of soldiers marched down the gangplanks and formed up on a field a short distance from the dock.

Liam's first impression of Florida was not a good one. He thought he had grown accustomed to the heat and humidity in Louisiana, but this was more than he expected. Liam supervised offloading the First Sergeant's and Company Commander's field desks and the boxes of papers, which are now organized and assembled correctly. The two Privates assigned to the task were none too happy being ordered around by another Private. When one of the Privates seemed to resent Liam's instructions, a quick "Do as you are told" by the First Sergeant put the young man in the proper attitude. Liam recognizes the authoritarian projection used by First Sergeant Harkins and files that away for possible future use.

After setting up Captain Gardiner's and First Sergeant Harkins' offices in the tents provided, Liam walked around his new home. He has spent the last four hours hot and sweaty with only a drink of water to cool him off. No longer the green recruit, but still unfamiliar with the Regiment's home in Florida, Liam's concept of a fort was limited to the walls and towers he knew in Ireland. Fort Brooke has none of that. Rows of tents, a dozen log cabins, and a single tower with a small structure at the top made up Fort Brooke. Liam soon learned that his company was reuniting with the other three companies of the 4th Infantry Regiment and that four companies had been stationed at Fort Brooke since 1828.

A benefit of being the company clerk was that Liam slept in the orderly room, the company's heart. Among his many duties was maintaining and performing daily upkeep on the small log cabin that was allocated to the company. Every morning at dawn, Liam folded up his cot, stowed his blanket and kit, and stood in the morning formation with the rest of the company. Once the formation was dismissed, he repeated his tasks of visiting each squad and prepared the morning report that First Sergeant Harkins reviewed and Captain Gardiner signed. For Liam, these were bookkeeping tasks that he mastered quickly. The correspondence that Captain Gardiner and First Sergeant Harkins generated kept him busy for the better part of the day.

Each week, when the company conducted its musket drills and fired, Liam joined his former tent mates in the first squad. The closer the squad came to the river, the more intense the mosquito bites became. The grim joke amongst the privates was that the mosquitoes were large enough to carry off a man. The local Seminole Indians showed the soldiers how to keep the mosquitoes away by rubbing garfish oil on exposed skin. The challenge for the soldiers was that the oil smelled so bad that they had to be infested with mosquitoes before they would resort to putting on the fish oil. Liam tried it once and was immediately reprimanded by First Sergeant Harkins for stinking like an Indian. "Wash yourself, Private" was delivered in no uncertain terms.

By late October 1837, the routine at Fort Brooke consisted of reveille, breakfast, morning drill, lunch, personal equipment maintenance during the hottest part of the day, afternoon drill, dinner, and some leisure time before last call and bed. First Sergeant Harkins is glad that he took Liam as the company clerk. He is impressed with Liam's efficiency and performance. He recommends to Captain Gardiner that Liam be promoted to senior private. Although it did not significantly increase his monthly pay, the single stripe on his uniform was a great source of pride for Liam. Unfortunately, it was also a source of irritation to Liam's former recruit tent mates. They saw him as the First Sergeant's favorite and his promotion as undeserved. Little did they know how hard the company's two leaders relied on Liam and how much clerical work he took off their schedules. This allowed the First Sergeant and the Company Commander to spend more time with the soldiers, molding them into a more efficient fighting unit.

Over four months, Liam had learned that there were two types of Seminole Indians: those who benefited from their association with the Army and those who resisted the Army's efforts to relocate them. Liam never learned the details of the First Seminole War, but some of the details provided by the older soldiers were gruesome. Stories of being impaled with spears, attacked at night, and stalking an enemy that seemed to disappear in the swamps gave the new soldiers much to think about.

Two clashes with the Seminoles provided proof of the tales told by the older soldiers. First Company sent two squads north to locate a civilian reported to have been attacked by the Seminoles. When they arrived at the cabin, two dozen Seminole warriors were waiting in ambush and wounded four of the soldiers before they could retreat to Fort Brooke. Regimental leadership recognized that small groups of soldiers were easy targets and determined to send out patrols of at least company size.

Liam wondered how he would respond if and when required to fight the Seminole. Little did he know that time was drawing near.

Chapter 11: Fighting the Seminoles

On December 23, 1837, First Company was ordered to accompany a supply and reinforcement march to Fort King, about 30 miles north of Fort Brooke. Major Dade, a staff officer in the Regiment, was designated as the detachment's commander. Captain Gardiner, commanding First Company, was second in command of the detachment. A detachment of 110 soldiers from the First Company, along with two wagons and their wagoneers, departed Fort Brooke in the late morning. Major Dade and Captain Gardiner were mounted while the soldiers marched in front and behind the wagons.

Captain Gardiner assigned Liam the task of inventorying the supplies taken to Fort King and accompanying the supply wagons. Liam had not participated in any engagements the regiment had with the Seminoles and viewed the trek to Fort King as an opportunity to see more of the country. Liam noticed that Major Dade carefully placed flank guards on both sides of the column when traveling through the thick woods and crossing the river. The first two days passed without incident. There were some reports of Indians shadowing the column, but none were more than an Indian or two.

An Irishman's Odyssey

On December 25th, Major Dade halted the column in the early

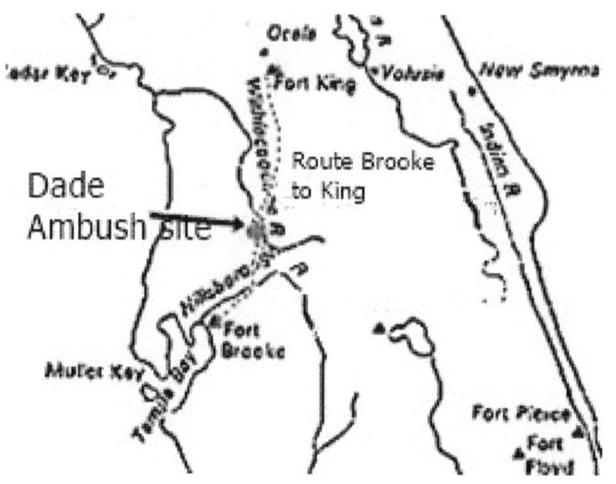

afternoon and allowed the soldiers to have a small Christmas celebration. The cooks made hot ham sandwiches on fresh bread, and potatoes and gravy supplemented the typical beans and bacon. Liam welcomed the warm food as it had become colder over the last few days. He and his fellow soldiers were grateful for their heavy woolen coats and fastened them close around their necks. Liam recalled how hot and humid it was when he arrived in June and found the cold all the more distressing. The ground alternated between wet and slippery to dry and dusty. Each soldier now had wet feet and a dusty overcoat.

The following day was slower than usual as they traversed multiple wet areas. Liam and other soldiers often had to push and pull the two wagons through the marshy swamp, which seemed to grab the wagon wheels and their boots. The only good thing about this time of year was that the mosquitoes were nowhere to be found, and most soldiers not on picket duty had a good night's sleep. On December 26, the column was on dry ground, surrounded by tall, thin pine trees and waist-high palmetto bushes. Major Dade pulled in the flank scouts, and the two columns of soldiers, with half in front and half behind the two wagons, continued their march. Liam and two other soldiers thought they saw Indians in the chest-high palmetto, but their warnings to the corporals and sergeants fell on deaf ears. Each soldier anxiously grasped his musket underneath his heavy wool coat. Liam wondered how they would retrieve their muskets from their coats if they had to fire them.

Just after a short break for a midday meal, Liam was close behind the second wagon. Within minutes of the column reforming and turning north, a shot rang out, and Liam saw Major Dade fall from his horse, almost certainly mortally wounded. Liam had not been fired upon before and was frozen in shock. He knew what had happened, but his mind could not comprehend it. He heard Captain Gardiner quickly order each column to face and raise muskets to the ready. Before most soldiers could raise their muskets from their heavy winter coats, a volley of over a hundred muskets tore through the column. Looking forward, Liam watched in horror as soldiers on his side in front of the wagon fell with wounds from more than one musket. Recovering, Liam pulled his musket from his coat and prepared to fire. As he looked beyond the smoke for a target, a second volley of an equal number of muskets fired directly at the soldiers around him. Liam felt a strong pull on his overcoat's left; a thump on his head knocked his cap off and turned him around as a musket ball shattered his musket stock in front of his chest. Liam, now unarmed, with blood running down into his eyes and shooting pain in his head, sags to the ground, sure he is mortally wounded. As he drifts out of consciousness, his last thoughts are of his beloved mother, Mary, Ireland, and Lucy, his first love.

Liam remained unconscious while the Indians stripped the wagons of supplies, collected weapons and ammunition from the dead and mortally wounded soldiers, and left with the four horses. Liam is left for dead as his head is covered in blood, and he is unconscious. When he recovers consciousness, Liam is confused, cold, and disoriented. The only sounds are those of birds he has heard for days. Eventually, he can stand and walk; he stumbles around the bodies strewn in front and behind the now empty wagons. None of the soldiers he checks are alive, and he soon abandons the hope of finding anyone alive. Still dizzy from his head wound and wandering aimlessly, Liam finds himself much distanced from the carnage he witnessed and sits against a pine tree to rest. The throbbing in his head is unrelenting, and he closes his eyes, hoping it will help.

Night has fallen as Liam awakens from his injury-induced sleep. He panics as he cannot see. His eyes seem glued shut. Panic grips him, and he cries and prays, "God help me, God help me." His tears gradually loosen the blood that has congealed on his face, and he can open his eyes. "How long have I slept?" he thinks. "The night is dark, and there is no moon. I have no idea how long it might be until dawn. What if the Indians come back? How can I defend myself?"

He is desperately thirsty, and his canteen is nowhere to be found. Unwilling to return to the carnage scene in the dark, Liam waits impatiently for dawn. At first light of dawn, Liam crawls slowly toward the bodies of his friends, now lying spread among the bodies of the rest of the column of soldiers. He remembered that Morrisey always carried two canteens. Hopefully, one has gone unnoticed by the Indians. Stumbling among the many bodies, Liam finds the bodies of his friends and sees that Morrisey is face down. Liam rolls him over and sees the canteen tucked beneath his coat. Liam brings the canteen to his lips, gulps down mouthfuls of water, and whispers,

"Thank you, God. Have pity on these poor souls. They did not deserve this death."

Resting his head between his legs, Liam cries for them and himself. Even when he fired for his life in Ireland, he has never felt so alone and vulnerable. Alone in the wilderness, somewhere between Fort Brooke and Fort King, and with only a vague idea of which direction each may be found.

Liam looks among the dead soldiers for anything that might be useful, but the Indians have stripped every one of them of anything useful. There are no bayonets, muskets, or bullets, and no more canteens. Some of the dead have been stripped of their boots and coats. Liam knows he must return to Fort Brooke and inform the regiment about what happened. If not, it may be days or weeks before their failure to arrive at Fort King is reported. As he thinks of his options, Liam sees that the trail they made arriving at this spot is clear and easily followed. Without further thought, he places the canteen strap around his neck and begins the long march back to Fort Brooke.

The first day was easy walking. The trail the column made in the pine needles is easy to follow. Although Liam's stomach growls often due to a lack of food, he knows returning to Fort Brooke is his only salvation. The second day is far more difficult. He is now in the swamp, and it has covered the tracks made by the wagon. There is little evidence that the column traveled through it less than two days ago. Liam has never felt more alone. The chaos of the ambush yesterday continues to dominate his thoughts. How could they have all been killed so quickly? How did he manage to survive when no one else did? He never had a chance to fire his musket. For that matter, He cannot remember ever seeing a Seminole. The ambush was well executed.

Liam stops often to orient himself and ensure he is traveling the right way. There is little more he can do than keep the sun to his right as he knows he must travel south to reach Fort Brooke. As night begins to fall on the second day, Liam finds a small hillock that is dry, surrounded by cypress stumps, and prepares to spend the long night alone again. His heavy woolen coat provides only a modicum of warmth, as nights in December can be decidedly cold. The sights and sounds of the ambush from yesterday continue to haunt his thoughts. Shivering with wet feet and pants, Liam falls asleep and dreams of warm coffee, fresh bread, and crisp bacon.

Chapter 12: Into the Wilderness

Liam awakens to the strong grumblings of an empty stomach. He knows he must conserve water, but wonders if he might find something to eat. Sipping slowly on his canteen, Liam wonders if he can reach Fort Brooke before thirst or hunger overtakes him. As the sun slowly breaks through the branches and reflects off the water around him, he struggles to regain confidence in his ability to follow the trail that was made three days ago. The water level in this part of the swamp seems higher now than when they crossed before. Does that mean he has lost the trail? If so, can he find it again? Those doubts swirl through his mind as he begins to walk what he hopes is south with the sun now on his left. Silent prayers for guidance and help provide support as he makes his way through the swamp.

At Fort Brooke, a Seminole who has worked as an Army scout learns of the attack on the column headed to Fort King. He knows only that the Seminoles fighting against the Army have declared a victory and are celebrating that success. Approaching the Regimental Headquarters, he sees Sergeant Major Makins and recognizes him as a senior regiment member. Carefully approaching Makins, the Seminole says quietly,

"I have learned that the soldiers sent to Fort King have been attacked by Chief Osceola and his Seminoles."

"What is that?" exclaims Makins.

"Army leader, I only know what I have learned from those who have family in Osceola's band. According to them, the soldiers have been attacked, and Osceola has been proclaiming a victory."

"When did this happen?"

"It would be three days past," says the Seminole.

"If you can learn more, you will be rewarded," says Makins as he hurries to the headquarters building.

Ignoring the protocol of knocking on the door of the Adjutant, Makins pushes in, "I have just learned that the column headed to Fort King has been attacked and may be in dire straits. The Colonel must hear what I have learned."

The adjutant knocks on the Colonel's door and enters without waiting.

"Colonel Hayes, you must hear what Sergeant Major has learned."

"Very well, Sergeant Major, what is so important?"

"Sir, I was approached by one of our Seminole scouts. He told me that the Seminoles, under Chief Osceola, had attacked our column enroute to Fort King. They are celebrating some victory from that attack. If that is the case, we may have wounded soldiers that need our help."

"Major, find Captain Smithers and Captain Jackson and have them come to my office immediately."

While the Adjutant is rounding up the company commanders of two regimental companies still at Fort Brooke, Colonel Hayes asks Sergeant Major Makins to identify those in the march and what was being carried in the wagons for Fort King. Learning that the number was over a hundred and the wagons carried much-needed supplies for Fort King, Colonel Hayes recognized that this was no accidental engagement by his soldiers and the Seminole. A veteran of the First Seminole War, he is well aware of Chief Osceola and his command over the Seminoles who oppose their relocation. This is the first significant engagement with the Seminole since the war with them ended with the Treaty of Moultrie Creek. Colonel Hayes is aware that the Seminoles were dissatisfied with the treaty's terms, and this is likely the first of many actions by the Seminoles.

Once Captains Smithers and Jackson arrive, Colonel Hayes asks them to estimate where the attack may have taken place, how many soldiers need to remain at Fort Brooke, and how many can be sent to the site of the attack. Smithers and Jackson agree that if the attack had occurred three days ago, it would have been on the third or fourth day of the movement to Fort King. It would depend upon how fast the column moved, but even at the fastest march, it would take a relief party two or two and a half days to reach the site.

Colonel Hayes orders Captain Jackson to take his company of 100 men and prepare them for immediate departure, ready to take on any Seminoles they may encounter. Having made the trip to Fort King once before, Jackson has his unit, Second Company, prepared to move by midday. Knowing the terrain he will cover and where the attack may have occurred, Jackson briefs his men on what to expect.

"The resupply convoy to Fort King has been attacked by bands of Seminoles led by Chief Osceola. Our mission is to move as rapidly as possible to the site of the attack, assist any of the soldiers who may still be there, and repel any further efforts by the Seminoles to interfere with Army operations in this part of Florida."

Each member of Second Company knows some of the soldiers in the column headed to Fort King and doubts they will find any alive. Veterans of the First Seminole War are familiar with the Seminole practice of killing prisoners. With grim determination, Captain Jackson leads his company on a forced march that he expects will find them near the ambushed convoy in two days. There are no complaints by the soldiers, with many seeking some revenge for what they assume is the death of many of their comrades.

Liam is out of water and has not eaten for 52 hours. He knows the swamp water will kill him if he drinks it, and none of it looks more than sludge. A vague recollection about a spring along their route four days ago spurs him on. Concentrating on finding his way through the swampy terrain has drained what little strength he has left. He tries resting more often to conserve the energy he has left. The acid memories of his brush with death and the sorrow for his lost comrades prey on his mind. Thoughts and flashes of his home in Ireland distract him.

Before he realizes it, the terrain has changed. He is no longer in the swampland but on dry, pine-needle-covered ground. Resting against a pine tree and hoping his trousers will dry, he hears the unmistakable sound of something splashing in water. Encouraged by the sound, Liam slowly walks toward it and finds tall fronds surrounding a clear pool of flowing water. The turtles that slipped off a log were the sounds he heard. Falling into the water face first, Liam drinks as much clean water as possible. Thirst quenched and canteen filled, he becomes acutely aware of the hunger suppressed by the need for water.

Liam's year in Florida has not provided much education on the territory's plants and animals. He recalls stories of veterans cooking alligators and other strange beasts, but he has no idea how he might catch them. Fish, he does know, and the water from the spring may provide sustenance. Scanning the spring and the water flowing out, Liam sees silver flashes in the sunlight and is sure there are fish. He remembers how he and Michael would catch fish in the small stream near their village. A simple channel for the fish to follow downstream, along with a weir or net to hold them in place, is all that is needed. Liam forages for sturdy branches that will support the weir he constructs. Stripping off his shirt, he tears it into strips and weaves them with broad leaves found along the slow-flowing channel. Once the weir is in place, Liam realizes he has no flint or steel to start a fire. He is not yet hungry enough to eat raw fish and remembers how he started a fire while hiding in the hills beyond his village. Dry firewood is abundant, and he needs little more than some crushed pine needles to use as tinder. Fashioning a bow from a green branch and a strip of his shirt, he soon can keep a dry stick moving quickly against the tinder, and a glowing ember rewards his effort.

With a fire going well and four cleaned and gutted fish on sticks against the fire, Liam now believes he might survive. He voraciously devours the two small fish he has cooked and empties his canteen. He lies down in a bed of pine needles and quickly falls asleep. The small fire keeps him warm for the better part of the night, and he awakens refreshed and confident. Two smaller fish provide breakfast, and as he refills his canteen, he regrets only that he has no coffee. Keeping the sun to his left, Liam gathers himself, pulls the overcoat around his chest, and heads south to Fort Brooke.

Captain Jackson and Second Company move north through heavy underbrush while Liam has his morning meal. The company has covered ten miles before stopping for the night. Captain Jackson has his sergeants pushing the men hard this morning, hoping that they will be within a day of the massacre site soon. Jackson is well aware that the Seminole will know the Army will send a force to the ambush site and has placed scouts ahead and on both flanks of the column. Coming onto dry forest land after a morning of wet swamp, a scout reports to Captain Jackson that he has detected a fire ahead. Wary that this might be a Seminole camp, Jackson sends five of his most experienced soldiers to determine the source of the fire. Advancing slowly through the pine forest, one of the soldiers quietly points to a murky figure moving through the woods. Hoping it might be a Seminole they can capture, the five quietly approach from three sides as the figure walks slowly but deliberately south. As the five can now see the figure more clearly, they notice it is wearing an Army greatcoat and carrying a small bundle. They see no weapons and prepare to capture the figure.

Liam has been walking for an hour and has kept a steady pace south. Unaware that the scouts of Second Company have observed him, he is shocked to find two soldiers with their muskets suddenly pointed at his chest in front of him. The soldiers are equally shocked to see a white man in a dirt-caked and frayed uniform coat, pants, and bloody rag-covered head. The senior member of the five scouts looks at Liam,

"Lad, who are you, and what has happened to you?"

These are the first words from another human being Liam has heard in three days, and he is dumbfounded. Staring at the five, he looks around and gasps,

"I am Private Liam Flaherty of First Company. We were attacked three days ago, and I may be the only survivor."

"We need to get you to Captain Jackson, Flaherty. We have been sent to relieve First Company on the march to Fort King. You are the first we have found."

Liam joins the five as they quickly move to join Captain Jackson and the rest of Second Company. News of Liam's discovery travels swiftly, and there are many curious stares as he and the five scouts make their way to Captain Jackson. Liam salutes Captain Jackson,

"Sir, I am Private Flaherty and was afraid I would never see another until now."

"Well, Flaherty, tell me what happened and how far we may be from First Company."

"Captain, it was over before we knew it. The Seminole fired two volleys before we could get off our first. The men in front of the wagons were down first. I was following the wagons, and the second Seminole volley took the rest of us down. I was struck three times. The ball that struck my head rendered me unconscious, and I guess the Seminole thought I was dead. When I regained consciousness, I could find no one alive in the company; the wagons had been stripped and the horses taken. The men had been stripped of muskets and equipment. I found only one canteen and was able to survive on it for the past three days. I reckon I have traveled two days from the site of the ambush."

"Well done, lad. See yourself to the surgeon and have him look at your wound. We need you to be with us when we reach First Company."

Liam spent the next hours with the regimental surgeon to have his head wound cleaned and bandaged. The company's First Sergeant provided Liam with a musket, powder pouch, replacement uniform, and cap. Now outfitted as the rest of the soldiers, Liam joined their march north. As they passed the tiny spring where Liam rested and refreshed, he thought how lucky he was to have found it. Without it, he may have perished.

The following day, the column moved steadily north to the site of the battle. No longer with a sense of urgency, the men of the company were not looking forward to their next task. Only Liam knew the full extent of the carnage they would find.

On the second day, the smell of death and the scavenger birds overhead clearly indicated they had arrived. Captain Jackson and his First Sergeant established multiple burial details, and the men went about their grisly task. Sorrowfully, Liam stood by as his close friends were laid in hastily dug graves. Few were untouched by scavengers, and having lain out for six days, most bodies were in a state of significant decay. The sound of shovels and bayonets scraping the ground was only interrupted by the occasional retching by more than one soldier. Just before the last sunlight left the sky, Captain Jackson noted that all the dead had been buried. He vowed that the soldiers would one day be recovered and provided a proper military burial. With no intention of staying the night at the site of the massacre, Captain Jackson marched the column north toward Fort King and an encampment away from the graves.

Chapter 13: Revenge is Never Sweet

Liam and Second Company arrived two days later at Fort King. Liam, the sole survivor of Second Company, 4th Infantry Regiment, has been instructed to remain with Second Company until First Company has been reorganized. Liam knows few soldiers from the Second Company, which adds to his melancholy. He feels guilty for surviving when so many did not. There is a growing need to do something about the death of his comrades. When talking with soldiers in Second Company, Liam learns that many of them are as focused on revenge for the killing of the First Company soldiers as he is. Unsurprisingly, three days after arriving at Fort King, three companies, the Second Company of the 4th Infantry Regiment and two companies of the 2nd Infantry Regiment, leave Fort King in search of Osceola and his band of Seminoles. A scout with the Army has located the main camp of Osceola and is confident that his band will be nearby.

After a day's march, the combined companies were near the location of the Seminole camp. Major Braxton, commanding the three-company detachment, calls in the three company commanders for a planning meeting. Seminole scouts have determined that more than sixty of Osceola's band are in the camp. The camp is bounded on the east by a river. Braxton places Second Company in the north, both companies of the 2nd Regiment in the south, and three field artillery pieces, with supporting infantry, are placed in the west. The field pieces are loaded with grapeshot and will fire on any Seminole attempting to escape to the west. The plan is to have the three companies advance on the camp and have the Seminoles surrender or face the muskets and artillery.

Liam finds himself on the right flank of Second Company and is just in sight of 2nd Regiment soldiers, who are 300 yards to his south. He sees the three field guns set up with the gunners prepared to fire. His nervousness is overwhelmed by his need for retribution. These are the ones who killed my friends. These savages stripped their bodies and even killed some of the wounded. With muskets ready and bayonets fixed, the line of soldiers advances on the Seminole camp.

The first volley of musket fire is directed at Seminoles attempting to charge the oncoming line of soldiers. As each line of soldiers is three deep, the volley from the first line is soon followed by a volley from the second and then the third line. Through the powder smoke, Liam cannot see a Seminole standing. As they stride further to the camp, Seminole bodies are found lying where they were struck down. Many have been struck multiple times, and there is blood everywhere. There are bodies of Seminole men and boys in mangled groups. Some are so torn apart they are near unrecognizable as human beings.

Captain Jackson appears through the now-dissipating smoke and exclaims, "Well done, men. We have Osceola and his warriors. The men of Second Company are avenged."

A loud cheer responds to Captain Jackson's announcement. Liam takes no joy in his second witnessing of what he now believes will become his life for the foreseeable future. There is no satisfaction in seeing the dead and dying Seminoles. They have suffered the same fate as his friends. For that, he is both glad and sad. He is glad because they have not had the chance to savor their victory weeks ago. Sad because he knows this will not be the end of the conflict. There are many more Seminoles and fewer soldiers, which portends a protracted war between them. Liam reservedly joins the celebrating soldiers on their march back to Fort King. In his gut, he knows this will not be the last bloody encounter with the Seminole.

The march back to Fort Brooke with Second Company is uneventful. After his return, Liam is called to the Regimental Adjutant's office and learns that he has been promoted to Corporal in the reconstituted Second Company. He is proud to have the two strips of infantry blue on his sleeve. At the same time, Liam is at first overwhelmed by his new  responsibilities with fewer than thirty soldiers, many of them recruits. He recognizes the many administrative tasks First Sergeant Harkins faced in a company of a hundred soldiers, as Liam has only thirty to look after. Liam also appreciates how Sergeant Jenkins' efforts to train Liam and his friends made them better soldiers. At the age of nineteen, Liam is responsible for training new soldiers into effective members of an infantry company. Working day and night, his thirty soldiers can soon march, fire their weapons, and move as a unit on the battlefield. Memories of his life before joining the Army are now only vague thoughts that he entertains before falling asleep. After ten months,

Liam's tenure in the reconstituted First Company is about to come to an end.

A renewed sense of urgency has been felt in Washington, and three additional regiments, comprising approximately 1,100 soldiers, have been dispatched to join the 4th Regiment. A general officer has been appointed as the commander of Army forces in the Florida territory. Major General Winfield Scott has fought against the Indians on the western frontier and understands the importance of experience in achieving success in battle. The 4th Regiment is directed to provide a small cadre of experienced officers and men to assist the three regiments that will be spread between Forts Brooke and King. As one of the more experienced junior corporals with battlefield experience, Liam is sent to the First Infantry Regiment as a squad leader. Upon his arrival at A company, 1st Infantry Regiment, the young company commander, Captain Austin, welcomes Liam and asks what his experience in Florida has taught him. Liam's response chills the young captain,

"Sir, the land will kill you as quickly as the Seminole. The Indians are brave warriors and should never be underestimated. If we are to prevail in any engagement, we must be firm and be prepared for the worst."

Austin asks, "Corporal, what has taught you these lessons?"

"Sir, if you will, I am the only survivor of the Dade Massacre of October last year."

"Well, Corporal, I believe you have much to share with the soldiers of A Company. You have been assigned to my company as a squad leader. That position requires a sergeant, and I am pleased to promote you to the status of brevet sergeant. You will wear the rank, and once you have successfully performed your duties for a year, the promotion will become permanent. From here on, you are the sergeant in charge of the 1st squad."

"Thank you, Sir. I will work to assist the company and, in particular, my squad in becoming the best in the regiment."

"I can ask no more, Sergeant Flaherty."

Liam asks one of the soldiers working near the commander's tent where he can find the 1st squad. His first impressions are not favorable. He notes that the tentage is poorly erected and aligned. The soldiers' uniforms are in poor condition, and he wonders what he will find when he inspects their muskets. He tells the first soldier he sees,

"Soldier, what is your name?"

"Scoggins, Sergeant. I am in the first squad. The six other soldiers you see are also members of the first squad. We have two soldiers on duty at the mess tent and one away on leave of absence."

"Scoggins, have the seven of you join me at the pine tree nearest your tent."

The seven soldiers mill around the base of the pine tree as Liam observes from a distance. He approaches them and commands loudly,

"Attention."

Each soldier comes to attention and looks straight ahead as Liam walks around the seven. Returning to the front of the seven, he commands, "At ease."

The seven soldiers move to the at-ease position and look quizzically at Liam.

"Men, my name is Liam Flaherty. That is Sergeant Liam Flaherty, and I am your squad leader. Do I understand that one of you is Senior Private Moore?"

A small, dark-haired youth who looks more or less full-grown responds, "It is I, Sergeant. I have been in 1st Squad since we moved here from Georgia."

"Moore, please tell me where you were trained and the status of 1st Squad's training."

"Sergeant, we all received our recruit training in Georgia, but we have received no training since arriving in Florida."

"Men, my first job is to provide the training you will need to succeed as soldiers in the 1st Regiment here in Florida. Our goal is to be the best squad in A Company and the 1st Regiment. To that end, we begin tomorrow by inspecting you and your equipment. As soon as you hear reveille and fall in with the rest of the company, I will be with you, and we shall begin. Do you have any questions?"

Scoggins raises his hand and asks, "Is it always this miserable in Florida? I seldom get a full night's sleep with the heat and the mosquitoes."

"Aye, July and August are the most miserable. For those reasons, having and using the proper equipment becomes your most important task. I shall move my tent nearest yours and look forward to meeting each of you after the evening meal. You are dismissed."

The following weeks are spent training his ten soldiers relentlessly. Captain Austin notes that the 1st Squad is always first on the shooting range and that its soldiers appear better dressed in uniform than their counterparts in the other squads.

In the Fall and Winter, the 1st Regiment engages in multiple engagements with the Seminoles, and A Company, with the 1st Squad leading, is the most successful in these encounters. Captain Austin sees Liam as a potential senior sergeant in the near future. Early in January 1841, Liam is called to Captain Austin's office, now a log cabin with two rooms.

"Sir, Sergeant Flaherty is reporting as ordered."

Stand easy, Sergeant. You are aware that First Sergeant Forrow has been hospitalized with malaria and is unlikely to return to the company. I need a First Sergeant who can command the respect of their peers and handle the administrative tasks required of the position. Are you that man? If so, I will promote you to Acting First Sergeant."

Liam is surprised. He has only been in First Company for eighteen months. He knows his squad is now the best in A Company and likely the best in 1st Regiment. He only became a full sergeant last year, and now he is being asked to take on the role of company first sergeant. Liam realizes he has been holding his breath. He quietly exhales and replies.

"Captain, I thank you for your confidence in me. I believe I can do as you have asked. I would be honored to become the First Sergeant of A Company."

"Then, First Sergeant, I suggest you find a good clerk and straighten out the mess left in Sergeant Furrow's absence."

"Aye, sir, that I will. I have my eye on a young private that should fit the bill. Corporal Moore should be promoted to Acting Sergeant and can lead First Squad."

"I trust your instincts, Sergeant Flaherty. We have much to do as the Seminole continues to be a challenge in this Florida territory."

As the company clerk in First Company, Liam knows what a First Sergeant's role and responsibilities. He learned well during his time with First Sergeant Hankins and Captain Gardiner and soon had the A Company orderly room operating as it should. Within a month, Captain Austin congratulated himself on selecting Flaherty as his new First Sergeant.

Chapter 14: Making the Army a Career

As the First Sergeant of A Company, Liam has a workload that consumes his time both day and night. Fortunately, he has a clerk who can now be trusted to complete the daily Morning Report. With that administrative burden somewhat relieved, he can concentrate on the day-to-day training regimen of the company and the supply needs of over 100 soldiers. Liam sometimes has to learn the hard way that not all sergeants or corporals perform to the highest standards he and Captain Austin are trying to establish.

In a telling moment, Liam finds one of his senior corporals in the kitchen staff stealing food and selling it to settlers outside Fort Brooke. Liam relied on the corporal to maintain the kitchen stocks, and his betrayal sours Liam's trust in the company's cooks. A short and decisive court-martial of the corporal sends the message to the rest of the cooks. Liam finds a corporal he trusts and assigns him as the head cook.

After a year as Acting First Sergeant, Liam is called into Captain Austin's office.

"Sergeant Flaherty, I commend you for your performance as Acting First Sergeant for the past year. The company has benefited from your leadership and exemplary performance as Acting First Sergeant. To that end, I am pleased to let you know that the Regiment has approved your full promotion to First Sergeant."

"Thank you, sir. It is an honor to serve as the First Sergeant of A Company. Our soldiers are among the best the Army has to offer and will continue the proud traditions of the regiment."

Only twenty-two years old, Liam now wears the three stripes below a diamond on his sleeve, the chevrons of a First Sergeant. The Army had adopted the insignia of First Sergeant as far back as 1777, and he is proud to wear it in the regiment.

Although most First Sergeants in the regiment are ten years older than Liam, officers and soldiers treat him with the same respect. Liam is nearing the end of his five-year enlistment and must decide whether to reenlist. He suspects the regiment's approval of his promotion is a sign that he should stay in the Army. In the spring of 1841, Captain Austin signed the reenlistment contract that Liam had executed before him. Having been sworn in as a naturalized American citizen by a magistrate at Fort Brooke a year ago, Liam now considers himself a career soldier.

For the next two years, A Company engaged in minor skirmishes with Seminole bands that continued to resist efforts to relocate them from Florida. Few soldiers were lost in the engagements, and Liam took pride in that accomplishment. Captain Austin attributed that success to the training and leadership of his First Sergeant. By the end of 1843, the conflict with the Seminoles had largely been resolved. The most significant number of soldiers lost in the intervening two years was from the 4th Infantry Regiment. Liam regretted not being able to lend a hand, but the leadership in the regiment had declined, and the loss of so many soldiers made that leadership void apparent.

Now privy to many of the decisions that influenced the Army's work in Florida, Liam was aware of the overall picture and why the Seminoles were being driven from Florida. Each week, more and more settlers arrived at Fort Brooke, and the road to Fort King was almost a highway. It was traveled daily by wagon trains of settlers. The few Seminole warriors that had not surrendered continued to be a nuisance along the trail. Company A was often tasked with providing security for these wagon trains during their travels.

On one company-size security detail, Liam found himself at the ambush site of four years ago. The smell of death, the screams of the wounded, and the abject fear of death all came unbidden to his senses. Turning to Captain Austin, he remarked,

"Captain, you know what this place is, do you not?"

"First Sergeant, I know it well. I suspect that there will be some memorial here for the soldiers who died on that day. Does the memory of that day continue to haunt you?"

"Aye, sir, it does. I knew but a few of them well, but I knew all of them. I shall likely never forget that day."

For the next four years, Liam excelled as Company A's First Sergeant, and the company was considered the best in the regiment. Captain Austin was promoted to Major and moved on to the Regimental staff. The new company commander, Captain John M.

Clendenin, was a West Point graduate, class of 1830. He had learned about First Sergeant Flaherty before joining the company and was eager to get to know him. Over the first months, the two established a solid foundation of mutual trust. Captain Clendenin relied on Liam to manage all the company administration and the training of the sergeants and corporals. He recognized that Liam was a natural leader and instructor and always encouraged him to extend his training throughout the company. As the weeks and months passed, Company A continued to lead the regiment in all respects. During engagements with the Seminole, Company A soldiers suffered the fewest casualties and inflicted the most casualties on the Indians. Within the regiment, it was clear that First Sergeant Liam Flaherty of Company A made the unit the leader in all categories.

Liam found that he relished the opportunities to lead soldiers and was good at the task. His encouragement of young soldiers was well known in the regiment, and young officers were often encouraged to emulate his leadership methods. Now a fully mature soldier, physically and professionally, Liam had little time for anything outside the company and the regiment.

Unbeknownst to Captain Clendenin, in the Fall of 1844, the Regimental Commander, Colonel Jack Johnson, was looking for a new Regimental Sergeant Major. Sergeant Major Moody was in his thirty-fifth year of service and had developed severe arthritis. He could no longer mount a horse and was often confined to his quarters. Reviewing the possible list of replacements, First Sergeant Liam

Flaherty was at the top of his list. Before making any decision, Colonel Johnson sat down with Sergeant Major Moody and asked for his honest appraisal of the First Sergeants in the regiment who might replace him.

Sergeant Major Moody knew his time in the Army and in the regiment was drawing to a close. He also knew that whoever took his place had a more significant role to play than he had been able to fill for the last year. After thinking a bit longer than Colonel Johnson expected, Sergeant Major Roger Moody replied,

"Colonel, you have seven company First Sergeants to select from. I doubt any candidates in the other regiments might be considered. So, if I may, I shall go through the First Sergeants in the regiment and give you my assessment of each. Let me start with the three who have just taken on their duties in Companies B, C, and F. They lack both the experience and the proven excellence you require. Now to the four others. First Sergeant Olson of Company D is the oldest of the three. He is not the best of the three and might be too old for the job. First Sergeant Withers of Company E is a solid performer, and I expect that in the future, he may become a Sergeant Major. From my perspective, he spends too much time in his orderly room and too little time training his sergeants and corporals. First Sergeant Gentry of Company G has a drinking problem. So far, it has not affected his performance, but many are aware of it.

Now, to First Sergeant Flaherty of Company A. He is the youngest of the seven, having been promoted to First Sergeant four years ago. However, he is a good leader, and his soldiers are, without doubt, the best in the regiment. He is a consummate instructor, and the results he produces are evident. If you select Flaherty, the only potential issue may be that the older First Sergeants feel overlooked and resent him. How he manages that will be a test for him, for certain."

"Roger, I value your assessment and will certainly consider all you have provided. Flaherty was at the top of my list, and I am pleased that we seem to share many similar views. We will shortly be moving the regiment west, and I need a Sergeant Major to manage that movement."

"Would you spend some private time with Flaherty in the next few days?" If I select him for the position, I do not want it to be a surprise, so you should inform him that he is being considered. His reaction to your conversations with him will tell me much about him before we meet later."

"Aye, sir, I would be pleased to carry out that duty. If you decide Flaherty is your man, I stand ready to provide all the assistance at my disposal."

"Sergeant Major, I would expect nothing less."

Over the next week, Sergeant Major Moody invites Liam to visit with him at Regimental Headquarters. At the first meeting, Moody looks across the room at the twenty-eight-year-old First Sergeant and wonders to himself,

"Was I ever that young? It seems so long ago." Turning to Liam, he asks, "Do you know why I have asked you to join me, First Sergeant?"

"No, Sergeant Major, I do not. I hope that is not something my soldiers have done that brings me here?"

"No, Flaherty. I have asked you to join me because Colonel Johnson and I have discussed who might be my replacement in the regiment. Your name was one mentioned. How would you like to be the Regimental Sergeant Major?"

The look on Liam's face is clear that he has never thought he might be the Regimental Sergeant Major. His stumbling reply is, "Sergeant Major, I am honored that my name has risen to a discussion with you and Colonel Johnson. My time with Company A has been a series of learning experiences I treasure. How might that allow me to be a good Sergeant Major?"

"Let us first discuss what you know about the job of the Sergeant Major. Do you have some ideas of what that role might be?"

"Some, Sergeant Major, but surely not all."

"For your education, I will summarize what my role has become. First, you are the senior enlisted man responsible for a regiment's discipline, management, and rosters. You are to advise the officers, and you are expected to be an expert in counting off the regiment and coordinating and attending regimental parades."

"Thank you, Sergeant Major. I had some idea of those responsibilities, but not all. Of them, which do you believe to be the most important?"

"Over my years, I believe the most important responsibility is to advise the Regimental Commander on the training, discipline, and welfare of the soldiers in the regiment. No one else will be closer to the Colonel than the Sergeant Major."

"Sergeant Major, with all due respect, how will the Colonel feel about a 28-year-old giving him advice?"

"Flaherty, I suggest you let the Colonel worry about that. If you fulfill the duties and provide the advice the Colonel needs, it matters not how old you may be."

"Thank you, Sergeant Major. May I discuss this with Captain Clendenin before giving my answer?"

"Certainly, Flaherty. It must, however, be between you and Captain Clendenin and no other."

"I will, Sergeant Major."

His walk back to A Company was filled with many thoughts. First, the awesome responsibilities of a Regimental Sergeant Major were ones Liam never expected would be his. He was comfortable as a First Sergeant, and moving to the leadership of the Regiment was a sobering thought. If he had learned anything from his previous experiences in leadership roles, it was that confidence and professionalism made all the difference. He knew that he had both the ability and the willingness to do the job.

Liam's conversation with Captain Clendenin went as he expected. Clendenin was sorry to see Liam leaving A Company but proud that his First Sergeant might be the Regimental Sergeant Major. The challenge for both Liam and his company commander was who would replace Liam as First Sergeant. While at least two senior sergeants might do the job, Captain Clendenin believed that only one was even close to Liam in his performance. After lengthy discussions, they agreed that Senior Sergeant Johnson would be Liam's replacement when and if the time came.

Sergeant Major Moody and Colonel Johnson had already decided that Liam would be the new Sergeant Major. Moody recounted his meeting with Liam and informed the Colonel that Liam had asked all the right questions and would be a suitable replacement. Colonel Johnson was pleased that Moody's assessment complemented his, and they discussed how best to announce a new Sergeant Major to the regiment. Most officers and Sergeants knew Sergeant Major Moody was expecting to leave the service. His physical limitations made it difficult for him to perform his duties, and there was an expectation that a new Regimental Sergeant Major would be appointed. The publication of Liam's promotion as the new Regimental Sergeant Major surprised many. The soldiers of A Company knew that Liam was the best First Sergeant in the regiment, and his promotion was celebrated. One of Liam's first duties was to organize the Regimental Parade for Sergeant Major Moody's retirement and departure. Wearing the rank of Sergeant Major was only uncomfortable for a few weeks.

At the parade to say farewell to Sergeant Major Moody, Colonel Jackson announced that the regiment would soon be embarking for Texas and joining the Army there. Newspaper stories of the many skirmishes with Mexican soldiers and the burning of some Texas towns along the border with Mexico were all the soldiers needed to know about Texas. Liam's efforts to keep the regiment focused on transporting almost a thousand soldiers, their equipment, and supplies occupied him for the following weeks. A strong relationship with the Regimental Adjutant made life a little easier.

After a leisurely boat ride across the gulf, Colonel Jackson and Regimental Sergeant Major Flaherty set up the regimental headquarters in a small adobe outpost outside a Brownsville settlement. Liam assumed this new theater of operations would require a level of small-unit leadership different from that in Florida. He soon learned his assumption was correct.

On April 25, a stunning defeat of a small US Army contingent along the Rio Grande River prompted a full declaration of war against Mexico by Congress. The 1st Regiment, the 3rd Infantry Regiment, and three artillery batteries were soon dispatched to support the major campaigns against the Mexican Army. The transition from an infantry regiment with few horses to an almost entirely mounted regiment took the companies several weeks to complete. Never more than an average horseman, Liam found his horsemanship improved the more time he spent in the saddle. Driving the First Sergeants of the seven companies to train their soldiers in a new type of warfare took far more time than he expected. Each ten to twelve-hour day was exhausting.

For the next two years, the 1st Regiment fought with distinction across the border with Mexico. Beginning with the Battle of Monterey, Liam was saddened to learn that Captain Clendenin was one of the first officers in the regiment to be killed in action in September 1846. In the battle of Buena Vista in February 1847, the regiment distinguished itself in an inconclusive battle with the larger army of Santa Anna. As Regimental Sergeant Major, Liam was instrumental in rapidly reassigning sergeants and corporals to units that had suffered losses. Colonel Jackson appreciated his knowledge and understanding of the individual leadership capabilities within the regiment. In many ways, Liam made both Colonel Jackson's and the Regimental Adjutant's jobs easier as he made it one of his primary responsibilities to know as many sergeants and corporals as possible in the regiment.

At the end of the war with Mexico in March 1849, Liam was a celebrated leader in the regiment and highly respected by the officers and soldiers. In July 1849, the regiment was directed cross-country to Jefferson Barracks, Missouri. The regiment's movement from Texas to Missouri took two months. Liam again found himself in the saddle every day, covering the movement of the regiment. Unbeknownst to anyone in the regiment, Liam celebrated his thirtieth birthday riding from one company encampment to another, meeting with the First Sergeants of four of the seven companies. He have even forgotten his birthday until after arriving at Jefferson Barracks.

Once the regimental headquarters was fully established, Liam met with Colonel Jackson.

"Sir, what might we expect in this next year? Are there campaigns further west we need to prepare for?"

"Sergeant Major, I have no idea what might be next. I believe the War Department and the Army have not yet fully understood what is to be done now that the fight with Mexico is finished. I do know that we will be here for only a short time, as much of the army is being sent west to protect settlers now moving westward. I am an old soldier and will shortly retire from active service. You, young man, have much to contribute to our Army. I trust you will give the new regimental commander the same support and counsel you have provided me."

"Colonel, it has been an honor to have served with you. The army is a better place for your service, and certainly, the 1st Regiment is better for it. When might we expect a new commander?"

"I expect you will see a new Regimental Commander sometime in the new year."

Chapter 15: Service and Promotion on the Frontier

Most of the Army's frontier forts were garrisoned by only one or two companies. The 1st Infantry's experience typified how the Army dispersed to cover the frontier. The regiment assembled briefly at Jefferson Barracks, Missouri, after returning from Mexico in July 1849. By 31 December, the regimental headquarters was firmly established at Jefferson Barracks. Company D remained at Jefferson Barracks, but Companies A, E, and K were at Fort Snelling, Minnesota; B and F at Fort Crawford, Wisconsin Territory; C at Fort Atkinson, Kansas Territory; G at Fort Leavenworth; and newly formed H Companies and I at Fort Scott, Kansas.

One of the determining factors of life in the U.S. Army on the American frontier was the small size of the force engaged in operations, often in relative isolation from the country and the rest of the Army. Scattered throughout hundreds of small forts, posts, outposts, and stations throughout the American West, often there was little more than a company of cavalry or infantry in each post. Liam soon realized that this isolation fostered a strong sense of camaraderie and bonding within the Army in a way that only shared suffering can. Officers and men often felt part of an extended family that had to look inward for strength, as it relied on its customs, rituals, and sense of honor, separate from the distant civilian world or even the very different military society "back East." This sense of unity, of "splendid isolation," kept the regiment and its companies together during the harsh missions of western frontier duty. At the same time, it often led to professional and personal stagnation. Promotion was slow, and chances for glory were few, given the dangers and hardships of small-unit actions against an elusive foe.

For the next two years, Liam spent most of his time visiting the companies and distributing the increasingly smaller number of corporals and sergeants necessary to keep each company functioning smoothly. The five-year enlistment for those soldiers who fought in Mexico had ended, and the regimental recruitment effort was falling short. Where the regiment once numbered almost a thousand soldiers, Liam could count no more than 600 soldiers scattered in isolated posts of 50-60 soldiers each in a company.

Liam shared the challenges his soldiers faced in the West. The few engagements with local Indians and the maintenance needs of multiple posts did nothing to increase the soldiers' capabilities or competence. The new regimental commander in the spring of 1851 made little improvement to the situation of the regiment. An officer older than Colonel Jackson obtained the command only because he was the most senior officer on the Army staff in Washington. He showed little interest in the welfare of the soldiers and seldom visited companies in the dispersed area of responsibility. His lack of combat experience was apparent when regimental officers came to Jefferson Barracks and attempted to explain why they could not safeguard settlers in such a vast wilderness. Worse yet was his complete disregard for Liam's advice and counsel on the status of the soldiers in the regiment. Liam spent less and less time at Jefferson Barracks and more time with the companies.

In 1852, the 1st Regiment received a new commander, Colonel Albert Johnston. Colonel Johnston, a veteran of the Mexican War, understood the regiment's mission and capabilities. He recognized that the dispersed commands required more leadership at the company level than ever. After visiting the units and assessing their strengths, he determined that replacing some leaders was necessary. Meeting with Regimental Sergeant Major Flaherty, he was struck by the depth and breadth of the Sergeant Major's knowledge and experience in the regiment. The most critical replacement was the leadership of C Company at Fort Atkinson in the Kansas Territory. On his visit to Fort Atkinson, Colonel Johnston found the company commander drunk and unable to lead his unit. To solve the immediate command problem, Colonel Johnston ordered Sergeant Major Flaherty to assume command of C Company and promoted him to Brevet Captain.

Liam fully appreciated the need to replace the commander of C Company but was surprised to be promoted and told to take command of the unit immediately. Quickly stripping his Sergeant Major stripes from his sleeve, he put the epaulets of a captain on his shoulders, took one of his most trusted sergeants, and headed to Fort Atkinson. Upon his arrival, he directed the still-drunken officer to return to Fort

Jefferson Barracks immediately, escorted by the trusted sergeant from headquarters.

Liam knew the First Sergeant of C Company. It was not his first meeting, and Liam could tell the First Sergeant was eager to please. The two lieutenants in the company were out on patrol and would likely not return for days. Fewer than thirty soldiers were living in the ramshackle buildings used as barracks. First Sergeant Baker, a thin German with almost as many years in the Army as Liam, was happy to see Liam as the new company commander. During that initial meeting, the First Sergeant described the poor morale, the lack of supplies, and the general malaise infecting the soldiers. Although he did not come right out and accuse the now-departed company commander of misusing funds, a quick review of the poorly maintained records indicated that something was amiss. Liam turned over all administration to First Sergeant Baker with a reminder that he would be monitoring often.

Upon his arrival, Liam held his first formation with his new command. As First Sergeant Baker assembled the soldiers before the flag pole, Liam watched each soldier respond to the First Sergeant's command. Conscious of the curious glimpses in his direction, Liam wasted no time marching to the front of the formation and commanding, "At Ease. My name is Captain Liam Flaherty. I am your new company commander. My mission is to help C Company become the best in the regiment in accomplishing our mission. I intend to do so by improving the conditions at Fort Atkinson and working with

First Sergeant Baker to ensure we can accomplish every mission here in the Kansas Territory. I know this fort is as close to a godforsaken place as any of you have ever been. However, it is our station, and we must do everything we can to make it livable so that we can accomplish our mission. I promise you that I will do everything possible to provide for each of you. First Sergeant Baker, take charge of the company and dismiss the men."

Liam saw his first task as improving the living conditions of his soldiers. He was surprised by how quickly they became "his" soldiers. The soldiers had constructed most of the barracks using local materials. They constructed jacal-type buildings in which cottonwood strips were tied together around a frame and filled with mud, clay, and grass, providing only rudimentary shelter from the elements. Winters and summers in Kansas can be brutal, and these shelters provided little warmth in the winter and were unbearable in the summer.

Before leaving Jefferson Barracks, Liam convinced the Quartermaster to give him funds to improve the Fort and a contract to construct adobe-style buildings. With the First Sergeant's recommendations on the company's most trustworthy corporals and sergeants, Liam pondered what tasks had the highest priority. The First Sergeant identified two corporals with experience in construction. After meeting with the two, Liam approached the local civilian leadership and sought workers with knowledge of adobe construction. Three men showed up the next day at Liam's office seeking work. Each had experience building adobe structures. Liam asked the two corporals with building experience to meet with the three workmen and devise a plan to construct proper Adobe-style barracks for the company. Jason Berger, one of the civilians, volunteered that he had been a foreman in a construction company and would, for extra pay, lead the construction process. Liam agreed and drew up a contract for the three to sign, with Berger as the foreman. Corporals Jones and Foster were detailed to the construction team and authorized to procure the necessary materials on behalf of the company. After carefully monitoring their purchases and work for three weeks, Liam was satisfied that the project was well and properly launched.

After days of eating poor-quality meals, Liam and the First Sergeant met with the lead cook and quickly recognized that the man was not up to the task. His excuses that he never had enough to provide for the soldiers fell on deaf ears. Liam again turned to the civilians working in and around Fort Atkinson for leads on kitchen staff. Within a day, Ling-Ling, a young Chinese woman, arrived at Liam's office. She was sent as an emissary of her parents, who operated a small diner in town and were willing to provide meals for the garrison in exchange for a guaranteed monthly payment and the use of C Company's kitchen. Before agreeing to the contract, Liam visited the small diner and asked for a meal. After enjoying the meal, he was assured that an agreement with the owner would meet the garrison's needs. Ling-Ling brought her parents and younger brother to Liam's office the next day and translated the contract for them to execute.

Ling-Ling was now a constant presence around Fort Atkinson. Liam enjoyed talking with her during dinner and was impressed with the family's journey from China to America. Over the next year, Liam and Ling-Ling became more attracted to each other. The conditions at Fort Atkinson left little time for intimacy or privacy, and Liam finally decided that a romantic relationship was impossible. With great regret, he spent a quiet hour in his office explaining his decision to Ling-Ling. She smiled, accepted his explanation, gathered herself, and returned to her parents' home outside the fort. From then on, whenever the two met, it was always a formal greeting and no small talk. Liam continued to write his mother monthly and was always pleased to receive her letters written in the graceful Spencerian script she practiced almost daily. He was careful about any relationship he may have had, and his mother was quick to inquire why he did not have anyone in whom he might have an interest. Her letters clearly showed that she did not want him to remain a bachelor for the rest of his life.

Once the necessary materials were gathered, the first building constructed was the kitchen and mess hall for the soldiers. Its completion and regular, well-prepared meals immediately improved the soldiers' morale and confirmed Liam's decision to outsource his needs. With the basic needs of shelter and food addressed, Liam turned to the unit's and its leaders' proficiency. Both Lieutenants were West Point graduates, and each suffered from a lack of good junior leaders in their squads. Liam spent weeks with each of them and their senior sergeants and corporals, developing and honing their needed leadership skills.

No longer were patrols sent indiscriminately across the company's area of responsibility. His experience in the Mexican War and with the Seminole taught Liam the importance of understanding his adversary to succeed. With the help of the Indian scouts assigned to the company, Liam developed a network of information gathering that allowed him to know where and when the Indians might attack wagon trains of settlers headed west. With that knowledge, the company was quick to deter attacks on settlers and those moving West through the area.

The Indians were only one of the many challenges facing the Army on the frontier. By 1855, Kansas had become a tinderbox with two rival governments existing in the territory, one pro-slavery, the other antislavery. The situation came to a head in May 1856 when proslavery forces sacked the town of Lawrence, Kansas, an antislavery, or free-soil, town. Several days later, the noted abolitionist John Brown and six of his followers retaliated by executing five pro-slavery men. The two events ignited numerous encounters between armed bands from both sides. For weeks, the two sides had been engaging in a series of attacks against each other. Lives were lost on both sides. In an unusual decision, the Governor of Kansas obtained permission to have C Company tasked to assist federal marshals in apprehending the parties responsible for the initial murders carried out by John Brown and his sons. Unfortunately, there was no love lost between the soldiers and those who supported the murderers. From that day forward, Liam sometimes faced open opposition to the missions assigned to his soldiers.

Between 1858 and 1861, Liam rode with patrols that operated between the warring parties to prevent a larger conflict. It seemed sometimes that his job, and that of his soldiers, was to act as a policeman between fellow citizens hellbent on destroying each other. The increase in travelers moving west was always a concern, and too often, the focus on the policing role detracted from the protection role the company was assigned.

As Liam sat on the porch of his headquarters building, gazing out at the barracks where his soldiers were stationed and reflecting on his years in command, he felt a mix of satisfaction and conflict. He was satisfied because he had accomplished everything he had planned upon taking command of Company C. However, he was conflicted because it seemed that there was no end to the outbreaks of violence in Kansas, and that he and his soldiers would be committed to this part of Kansas for many years.

No longer the red-headed Irish teenager from County Kilkenny running from the constables, Liam was now a United States citizen and an officer in its Army. Years on the frontier had hardened him in more ways than he would have imagined twenty years ago. He had seen many soldiers, Indians, and settlers die. He had also seen the selfless courage of soldiers under some of the most desperate circumstances and the stubborn resiliency of settlers in this harsh land.

He had also come to appreciate the resolute and often stoic Indians of the plains. He found that once they made an agreement, they kept their word. Only white men broke the treaty or contract. Liam often shared his views of the Army on the frontier in his monthly letters to his mother. Her letters reflected optimism for Liam's safety, which he felt may be misplaced.

At thirty-six, Liam has almost twenty years in the Army, the last six of which are as a commissioned officer. The rumblings brought on by the conflict between proslavery and antislavery forces in Kansas presage a conflict between states that hold very different views on both states' rights and slavery. If that conflict should come, Liam knows officers from the South who are ardent states' rights and slavery proponents and officers from the North who are dedicated to antislavery. Their differences seem irreconcilable. Liam can only guess how the regiment and the Army may be divided should a war between the states unfold. He knows Colonel Johnston is from Virginia and will almost certainly follow his state's lead.

Liam has seen too little of the slavery that many in the antislavery groups object to and finds little to justify the ardent proslavery groups. He understands economic slavery as practiced in Ireland and is, by nature, antislavery. Careful to keep his views on slavery close, Liam sees many in his company now separated by their opinions.

His worst fears about a coming conflict will soon be realized.

Chapter 16: War Between the States

The election of Abraham Lincoln in the Fall of 1860 seemed to Liam to be a pivotal time. One of his lieutenants and Colonel Johnston resigned their commissions and returned to Virginia, one of the first states to secede from the Union. Liam did not learn that armed conflict had started in South Carolina in April 1861 until later in June. In his heart, he was saddened to learn that Americans were actually at war with each other. While he was not a staunch antislavery officer, he believed that slavery did not fit well with the America he had adopted as his country. Many of the officers in the regiment had hoped that the conflict in the east would be contained there.

With the departure of many officers and senior sergeants in late 1860 and early 1861, the regiment required reorganization. The Army regiments west of the Mississippi were often understrength, and recruits did not join the Union Army in Kansas. In the reorganization, Liam relinquished command of C Company to a seasoned Lieutenant, was promoted to Brevet Major, and assumed the duties of Regimental Adjutant. Liam was sad to leave the company, and He realized that as the most senior Captain, his role in the regiment would have to change. Soon, the 1st Regiment received orders to move west and join Brigadier General Nathan Lyon's Army of the West at Springfield, Missouri. Undoubtedly, the conflict that began in the East would now engulf Kansas and Missouri.

Brigadier General. Nathaniel Lyon's Army of the West was camped west of Springfield. Within days of the regiment's arrival, 1st Regiment scouts identified Confederate troops near Wilson's Creek, about 12 miles southwest of Springfield. On August 8th, Regimental Adjutant Brevet Major Liam Flaherty accompanied the new Regimental commander, Colonel Bremerton, to a meeting with Brigadier Lyons and Colonel Sigel, 5th Regiment Commander. The plan was for Lyons to lead with two columns, one on the right flank commanded by Colonel Bremerton and one on the left flank by Colonel Sigel, to attack the Confederates on Wilson's Creek. Liam rode with Colonel Bremerton back to the headquarters, where they reviewed the plan of attack with the seven company commanders. The plan of attack for the 1st Regiment, now only seven companies, was for companies A and B, to lead with D and F behind and C and E and G in reserve.

At 5:30 on the morning of August 9th, Companies A and B hit the Rebel cavalry hard, and the Confederates fell away from the rise, soon known as Bloody Hill. Confederate forces quickly rushed up and stabilized their positions on the hill. Within hours, Confederate infantry counterattacked the Union forces, hitting both the 5th Regiment's and 1st Regiment's lines three times that morning. In each, they failed to break through the Union lines. Brigadier Lyon was too close to the front lines and was killed during the third Confederate counterattack, and was replaced by Colonel Bremerton. As the ranking 1st Regiment officer, Liam assumed temporary command of the 1st Regiment. He moved quickly to reinforce the lines held by D and F Companies and placed C and G Companies immediately behind the four forward companies. He rode continuously up and down the regiment's line, encouraging the soldiers and directing the fires when necessary. He watched as the Confederates routed Sigel's column south of Skegg's Branch. By the end of the third Confederate attack, which ended at 11:00 am, three of the 5th Regiment's companies pulled back. Sigel realized his men were exhausted and his ammunition was low, so he ordered a retreat to Springfield.

Liam ordered A and B companies to move to cover the 5th Regiment's retreat. Before any significant exchange of fire took place, it was apparent that the Confederates were too disorganized and ill-equipped to pursue. With that lull, Liam ordered his companies to consolidate and move quickly to support the 5th Regiment as it moved back to Springfield. The 1st Regiment suffered over twenty killed and more than thirty wounded. Except for the few veterans from the Mexican War, like Liam, none in the regiment had experienced such losses. He instinctively knew how difficult it would be for the soldiers. Colonel Bremerton remained in command of the Army of the West and was promoted to Brevet Brigadier. In recognition of his performance in the first major battle of the Civil War in Missouri, Liam was promoted to Brevet Colonel and was to remain in command of the 1st Regiment. In his first meeting with his company commanders, Liam told them they had done well at Wilson's Creek. Their companies held the line, and if the 5th Regiment had been able to do the same, the combined force may have prevailed that day. The 5th Regiment's withdrawal was necessary, and it did not reflect on the valor and performance of their companies. The proficiency and valor of the 1st Regiment in its support of the 5th Regiment were testimony to the leadership and training they had received. To the credit of their officers and noncommissioned officers, the soldiers' training was evident.

Unfortunately, the Confederate victory at Wilson's Creek buoyed southern sympathizers in Missouri and sustained the pro-slavery Missouri State Guard activities. Wilson's Creek, the most significant 1861 battle west of the Mississippi River, gave the Confederates control of southwestern Missouri. The 1st Regiment participated in multiple minor engagements with Confederate units for the next four months. In each Brevet Colonel Liam Flaherty was at the center of the fight and was recognized twice for his courage and stalwart leadership under fire.

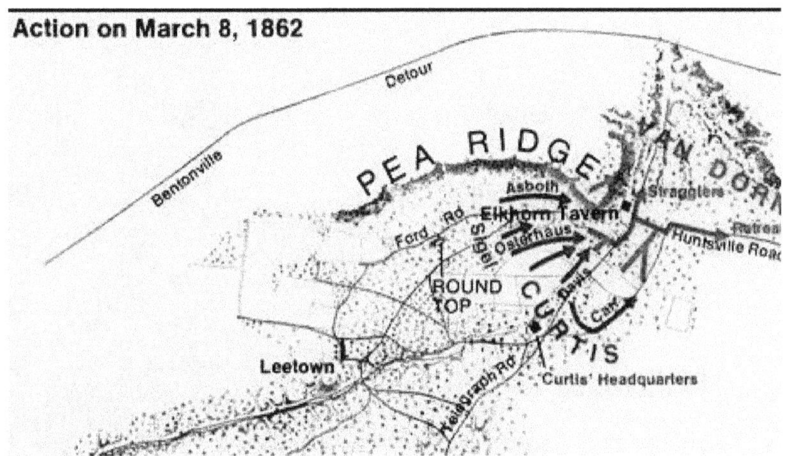

An Irishman's Odyssey

In March 1862, the Union Army sought to clear secessionist forces from Missouri. The 1st Regiment joined Union General Samuel R. Curtis's forces as they pursued Confederate General Sterling Price into northwest Arkansas. On March 7, the 1st Regiment was among the Union forces attacked by the combined Confederate forces of Price and General Ben McCulloch. Named later as The Battle of Pea Ridge, the conflict commenced east of Bentonville, Arkansas, with the Confederates attempting to outflank Curtis's Union forces. On March 8, Liam led the 1st Regiment's counterattack as part of Davis's Division and achieved a decisive victory. General Curtis recognized the key role of the 1st Regiment in the attack and extolled the capabilities of its commander, Brevet Colonel Liam Flaherty. Although the battle was an essential early turning point in favor of the Union, secessionist bushwhackers and Confederate raiders presented an ongoing threat to Union control in Missouri and Kansas in 1863 and early 1864. Although none of the engagements with bushwhackers were significant, they kept the soldiers of all 1st Regiment companies actively patrolling. The final major engagement of 1864 was at Mine Creek in October, where the 1st Regiment, now part of a mounted provisional cavalry division, defeated the cavalry of Confederate generals Marmaduke and Fagan. The loss of 1200 Confederates, of which 600 were captured, effectively ended any significant Confederate efforts in the southwestern theater. The 1st Regiment remained part of the Army of the Southwest for the remainder of the war as Union forces maintained formal military control of Missouri and most of the western side of the Mississippi.

Multiple minor engagements between the Army and scattered Confederate units had little impact on the control of Kansas. Liam worked tirelessly to manage the many 1st Regiment engagements and found himself in the saddle for more than ten hours each day. When word of the Confederate surrender at Appomattox reached the units in Missouri, Liam and the 1st Regiment were still chasing Indians and bushwhackers. To Liam, the event in Virginia seemed to have no relevance to what the Army was doing in Missouri and Kansas.

Soon after the end of the Civil War. The Army in 1865 had become a shadow of its former self in less than a year. Half of the soldiers in the 1st Regiment left the Army and returned home. Where Liam once had ten companies, there were now back to the prewar five, and they were short of experienced sergeants and corporals. Like the Army's reduction in size, Liam had been reduced in rank and was again a Major, but still in command of the regiment. By early 1866, the regiment was scattered across western Kansas, as it had been before the war, fighting Indians and securing the movement of more settlers west. It seemed to Liam that armed conflicts with Indians, between settlers, or between settlers and Indians were the never-ending story of the Western frontier. He was fortunate to have an adjutant and sergeant major who handled the regiment's administrative details, allowing him to spend time with the companies. Instinctively, he recognized good leaders and did all he could to keep them in important positions. Some officers felt he was too concerned with individual leadership and too harsh with those who did not meet his high standards. Liam knew how some in the Regiment felt, but relied more and more on his ability to recognize the leadership qualities needed for success in the Regiment's missions.

In January 1867, Liam returned to Jefferson Barracks, where he had started almost twenty years before. Now he occupied the office of the Regimental Commander. With over 20 years of service in the Army and the last eleven years as an officer, he has had limited opportunities to meet women and, consequently, has never been married. Always frugal, a portion of his salary has been deposited monthly in a bank account in Kansas City for the past twenty years. His mother's letters paint a rosy and optimistic picture of Ireland. She never asks for money, but Liam sends some each month anyway.

The Army has been his occupation and life since joining as a teenager. All he knows is the Army and soldiers. What can he expect in the Army for the foreseeable future? At 49, he is much younger than many of his counterparts in command of infantry regiments. With no experience outside the Army, is there a future for him in the Army? Unsure of what that future may be, Liam writes a long letter to General Curtis, who commanded the Army of the Southwest. Liam knew Curtis considered the 1st Regiment and Liam, one of his best leaders. In the letter, Liam sought General Curtis's views on what the Army would be doing in the next decade and whether there would be a future for officers like him. General Curtis's reply took three months. When a clerk brought Liam the envelope, he laid it on his desk without opening it. He knew that the response to his questions would determine the next chapter of his life.

Liam reflects on his service in the United States Army. He is a little surprised that he has not suffered a serious wound, major illness, or injury. Reflecting on this good fortune, he cannot help remembering all those who served with him who did not have his good fortune. He remembers Captain Clendenin fondly, who fell at Monterey. He was one of many who passed through Liam's life as a soldier.

Chapter 17: An Unknown Future

With a small glass of his favorite whisky in hand, Liam opens General Curtis's response. The flowery compliments given to the regiment and his leadership are accompanied by descriptions of a rapidly shrinking Army and limited advancement opportunities for many. Although Curtis did not say it, it was clear to Liam that without social and political connections, there was little chance of his either staying in the Army or advancing. Curtis concluded his letter by wishing Liam well and asking him to continue the good work the regiment is doing in Kansas. Liam learned later that Curtis's letter was one of the last he ever wrote. Samuel Curtis died in late 1866. Liam took Curtis's letter stoically, recognizing that his situation differed from that of many other officers. They had family or professions that would welcome them back to the fold. He had neither and had to decide what to do for the rest of his life. For the first time in many years, thoughts of Ireland became more than just casual remembrances. Liam's memories of Ireland were those of a teenager with a loving mother, friends, and a community he was familiar with. The green hills and pleasant weather he remembered contrasted with the heat of a Kansas summer and the cold of a Kansas winter.

Over the years, Liam's only contact with Ireland was the occasional letter from his mother, Mary. Ever the optimist, she relayed little of the turmoil that gripped Ireland years after Liam's departure. His contacts with Irishmen who recently immigrated to America gave Liam a limited perspective on how his part of Ireland had changed.

One young man who left in 1854 recounted events during what was described as "the Hunger," or the Great Irish Famine, which began in 1845. What he did not know was the effects that famine continued to have on those still in Ireland. Liam was also unaware that in the late 1860s, Ireland experienced a rebellion against British rule. The Irish Republican Brotherhood (IRB), also known as the Fenians, had organized an unsuccessful revolt against British rule earlier in the year. The population of Ireland continued to decline after the Great Famine, which is often considered to have ended in the late 1850s. Ireland continued to experience a decline in manufacturing, resulting in fewer job opportunities for those seeking employment. Only the brewing and distilling industries, the major employers in Dublin, continued to thrive. The issue of land ownership remained contentious. Many farmers joined the Irish National Land League to advocate for lower rents and greater land ownership. All of these had a major impact on the Ireland that Liam remembered. Some he would come to learn personally when he returned to Ireland.

Eager to learn more about his long-forgotten birthplace, when Liam now wrote to his mother, he asked questions about the village, his friends, and, in particular, those who had helped him leave Ireland. Her always optimistic responses gave Liam hope that a return to Ireland might be the better option for his future. Mary Flaherty included a brief letter from Father Murphy, not long after Liam received General Curtis's response. Father Murphy provided a more realistic view of what Liam might experience if he were to return. As a teenager, Liam had considered Father Murphy an old man at twenty-five. Murphy had been the village priest for 35 years, and at 60, he was still an active and enthusiastic parish priest. He remembered Liam quite well as one of the few he encouraged and helped leave Ireland. The circumstances of Liam's departure in 1832 were far different from those who had no choice but to leave Ireland in the early and late 1850s. Father Murphy recounted the struggles endured by the community, primarily the turmoil caused by the IRB in its efforts to overthrow British rule.

While Father Murphy encouraged Liam to return to support his mother, he warned that the IRB was actively recruiting Irish veterans of the American Civil War. Unfortunately, some who had declined the invitation to join were beaten, and more than one mysteriously disappeared. Liam was familiar with the outlaw former Confederate soldiers who required the attention of the Army when they were criminally charged. He knew how to deal with them, but members of his community actively moving against the English crown was a different matter. How might he deal with that if and when he returned to Ireland? It would have to wait. The mission of the Regiment came first, and plans to leave the Army and return to Ireland would have to be put on hold.

Within the month, Liam was forced to make a decision. In its infinite wisdom, the Army decided to retire the 1st Regiment and incorporate its companies into the newly formed Army of the West, with headquarters in California. When he inquired about his next assignment, Liam learned that Majors were in such ample supply that the Army no longer needed that many. As one of those no longer required in the Army, Liam could petition to return to his original rank and stay in the Army or retire as a Major. With no desire to return to his Sergeant Major rank, Liam formally requested that he be retired from the Army as a Major for pension purposes and formally retain the rank of Colonel after retirement. The letters and documents formalizing the transfer of the companies and Liam's retirement took more than two months.

In the Spring of 1868, Liam stood on the parade ground with the soldiers of the 1st Regiment. The Regiment's colors were cased and retired. Orders were read, assigning the six companies to the Army of the West and the 5th Regiment. The final set of orders read was those announcing the retirement of the Regimental Commander, Colonel Liam Flaherty. After the Regiment had passed in the parade and the soldiers of the Regiment moved to their barracks in preparation for the move west, each officer approached Liam, saluted, and offered their best wishes. Liam returned to his headquarters, where he and his Sergeant Major shared a long drink of his favorite whisky, reflecting on their time together.

"Colonel, what plans have you made for your departure from the Army and Jefferson Barracks?"

"I have made but a few. I will be moving to Kansas City tomorrow. I have booked a room at the hotel. From there, I might travel to Ireland and visit my mother, but I have not yet planned to do that."

"I hope you know, Sir, that the officers and men of the Regiment hold you in high regard. Those who have served with you for years, as I have, believe there is no better Regimental Commander."

"Sergeant Major, I take that as the highest compliment I could receive from those serving with me, in this Regiment or any other."

With those final words, the Sergeant Major gives Liam his most professional salute and strides purposefully out the door.

The following morning, a wagon with two trunks containing Liam's worldly belongings follows Liam from Jefferson Barracks to Kansas City. Riding his horse in civilian clothing for the first time in a long time, Liam finds it strange that there are no soldiers to accompany him. For the past ten years, he has never marched or ridden alone. The amusing thought that passes through his mind is that the private driving the wagon hardly constitutes a military escort. Liam realizes he is alone for the first time in more than twenty years and will likely be that way for some years to come. Two days later, the wagon and Liam arrive in Kansas City, and Liam takes residence in a small apartment in the newly built Pacific House Hotel. The proprietor recognized Liam as the Colonel of the Regiment and provided the hotel's best accommodation.

After dinner, Liam returns to his room. Now, what do I do, keeps running through his mind. I know no one in Kansas City. I have few friends here in the United States. Most of those I have served with are scattered across the states or dead. While many might welcome a visit, none need a retired officer. Any skills I have are of little use in the civilian world. With my savings and a small pension, I might consider starting my own business, but I'm unsure what that business would be. Returning to Ireland and visiting my mother might help me focus on the following years. Since the Tithe Act was repealed and the Articles of Redemption approved by the Irish Parliament, there is no longer any reason why he could not travel to Ireland. With that decision made, a plan is devised on how best to leave the United States for Ireland.

For the next three days, Liam will be at the telegraph office making arrangements to travel to Charleston, South Carolina, and embark on a transatlantic voyage to Liverpool and Ireland. The new steamship Baltic promised a trip of no more than two weeks. Liam was looking forward to the sailing, remembering his life aboard the Primrose and its fifty-day voyage from Liverpool to New Orleans. The train travel from Kansas City to Charleston required Liam to change trains only once, in Cincinnati, for a brief stop of a few hours. Liam enjoyed the trip more than expected, as it was part of America he had never seen before. He took in the abundance of trees and well-kept farms along the rails and was reminded again how fortunate he was to have become a citizen. Many of them reminded him of the farms and villages in County Kilkenny.

Arrival in Charleston was another eye-opening experience. The harbor was larger than Liam had ever expected. The number of steel-hulled, smoke-belching ships in the harbor was almost too many to count. The few three and four-masted actual sailing ships were outnumbered by half.

Liam had booked a first-class ticket and was pleased to see his cabin was all he expected. A nice bed, a compact desk, and a water closet next door were all new, bright, and shiny. Just as he was putting his clothes away, there was a knock on the door. When he opened the door, a bearded, sharply dressed officer stood before him.

"I understand there is an Irishman aboard named Liam Flaherty. Is that you by chance?" Says the sailor.

"I am Liam Flaherty. Why is it, you ask?"

"I suspect you do not remember me, Liam, or was it Michael?

"Jamie Watkins! Is it you?

"Aye, it is, and welcome to my ship. I am the captain of the SS Baltic. A bit different than the Primrose, eh?"

With that, Jamie steps into the cabin and embraces Liam. The two slap each other on the back and remark how well each has weathered the many years since they sailed together.

"Jamie, can we spend some time together and catch up? In thirty years, much has happened to both of us."

"We shall, Liam. I expect a ten-day journey to Liverpool. It will give us some time to renew our friendship and catch up on the years that have passed. Now, however, I must return to the bridge and see to it that we leave Charleston Harbor on time and in the best manner. I still haven't forgiven you for leaving me alone on the Primrose with that scoundrel, Turnbull."

As he marveled at the coincidence of traveling back to Ireland on a ship captained by his old friend, Liam went to the first-class lounge. The process of the crew embarking the remaining passengers and loading the final bales of cotton cargo held his attention. A woman, standing not far from Liam and looking at the same scene, remarked to no one in particular,

"It seems a large crowd of people. Where will they all stay on the ship?"

Liam noticed her for the first time and responded, "There is room for many in the cabins below deck. Those are pretty small, and the accommodations are much less."

As she turned to his voice, Liam saw a dark-haired woman with sparkling grey eyes and an impish smile. Immediately, her beauty and her self-confidence struck him. Almost as tall as Liam, she confidently smiled at him and asked,

"And how might you know that, good sir?"

"Having sailed as a lad from Liverpool, Madam, I am familiar with the spaces available on most ships, and ours can accommodate almost 200 passengers. May I introduce myself? I am-" he almost said Colonel, but continued, "Liam Flaherty, at your service."

"Have we met before, Mr. Flaherty?"

"I think not, madam, as I am certain I would have remembered."

"Then, Mr. Liam Flaherty, I am Mrs. Lucinda Mayhew Poitier."

"It is a pleasure to make your acquaintance, Mrs. Poitier. May I assume you are traveling to England to visit London?"

"No, Mr. Flaherty. Liverpool is but my stop before traveling further to visit family in Ireland."

"Then we have something in common: I will also travel to Ireland to visit family and friends. Where in Ireland will you be traveling?"

"My family is originally from Queens County, and I will be visiting my grandparents at home in the town of Maryborough. I have visited them only once before and wish to see them again."

"As I do not detect any Irish in your speech, when did you leave Ireland?"

"I never left Ireland. My parents left more than forty years ago, and I was born in Charleston, grew up there, and was married there. My husband was a proud South Carolina officer who fell at Chancellorsville, Virginia, while serving under General Lee. And you, sir, what are your Irish roots?"

"I left Ireland as a young man thirty-plus years ago and will visit my mother, Mary, in County Kilkenny. I have not yet decided how long I will stay or how I shall manage our small piece of land if I do stay. May I offer my condolences on the loss of your husband? We all lost too many fathers, husbands, sons, and brothers in that awful conflict."

"Thank you, Mr. Flaherty. Did you participate in the war?"

"I did. My service was in the west, and we fought the Indians as much as we fought each other. Some of my closest friends were lost on both sides."

Liam is intrigued by this woman and feels compelled to spend more time with her.

Lucinda is drawn immediately to this Irishman. His demeanor speaks volumes about the life he has experienced, more than she can see. She is a product of her upbringing in the wealthiest South Carolina society. Yet, this man intrigues her as no other since her husband's departure for war. She decides she must know more about Mr. Liam Flaherty. Almost as if he has read her thoughts, Liam asks,

"As we have much in common, Mrs. Poitier, may I ask you to join me for dinner tonight?"

"You may, Mr. Flaherty. I would be pleased to join you for dinner."

"I suggest we meet in the first-class dining room at 7."

"I shall see you there."

Unbeknownst to Liam, Captain Jamie Watkins has sent an invitation to Liam's stateroom, inviting him to join him at the Captain's table for dinner that evening.

Summoning the steward, Liam quickly penned a request to Jamie that Mrs. Poitier accompany him to dinner. He then wrote a note to Mrs. Poitier, requesting that she join them at the captain's table for dinner. He explained that the Captain was an old friend and had extended the invitation to both of them.

Chapter 18: An Unexpected Travel Companion

Liam met Mrs. Poitier at the entrance to the dining room. Her beauty and poise struck Liam again. As she took his arm, they were shown to the Captain's table. The two other couples at the table were delighted to be introduced to them. Mrs. Poitier had met one of the other ladies earlier and recognized her from Charleston high society events. Liam was initially at ease, having spent little time at formal dinners during his time in the Army. Careful to watch Mrs. Poitier during the dinner, he found himself increasingly impressed with her bright personality and intelligence.

Jamie was an entertaining dinner host. He quickly put everyone at ease by telling the story of how he and Liam sailed together from Cork and how Liam abandoned him in New Orleans. The conversation around the table was anything but boring, and Liam learned that Lucinda Poitier's family had prospered in Charleston and that her father was now one of the wealthiest in South Carolina. Two of the dinner guests were familiar with Lucinda's father and praised his community involvement and support for the arts. Liam remembered young Mark Ketchum's father in New Orleans, and how successful he had been in receiving and shipping incredible amounts of cotton to Europe, one of the most profitable businesses in the South, both before and during the Civil War. When the other dinner guests learned that Liam had been the commander of the 1st Regiment in some of the most decisive battles of the Civil War, he was no longer just Captain Watkins' friend and guest. Captain Watkins's commentary on Liam's role as a deckhand was amusing and instructional. Liam reinforced Captain Jamie's comments by insisting that he would indeed have been dropped at the port of Liverpool had Jamie not been such an excellent teacher and friend. Jamie also reminded the guests that Liam had jumped ship in New Orleans, leaving him at the mercy of disgruntled sailors.

Liam was surprised that Lucinda did not act like many of the privileged, wealthy people Liam had known. Instead, she was a down-to-earth, genuine person whom Liam was increasingly drawn to during the dinner. Lucinda, in turn, was fascinated by Liam's story of his journey from Ireland to America. Liam's service in the Union Army seemed irrelevant to Lucinda as she knew Charleston men who chose the Union and not the Confederacy. As the child of wealth, Lucinda knew only those in her parents' circle of friends, schoolmates from the same social circles, and the other wives of Confederate officers who were awaiting their husbands' return. Unknown to Liam, as their only child, Lucinda's father was grateful to see her marry well. He provided a substantial dowry that was passed to her upon her husband's death. Lucinda was now the sole beneficiary of her and her late husband's wealth.

As Liam told how he traveled from his home in County Kilkenny to Cork, then from Cork to Liverpool, and finally to New Orleans, Lucinda learned that the world was far different from what she knew. Liam's experiences were so unique to Lucy that she wanted him to expand on them so that she could better appreciate them. He was also a handsome man, his red hair now touched with grey at the temples.

At the end of the dinner, Captain Watkins bid them all farewell. As he left, he asked Liam to join him on the bridge at his earliest opportunity. As politely as he could, he told Mrs. Poitier he would be joining the Captain and must say goodnight. She looked disappointed and said that it had been an enjoyable evening and dinner. Encouraged by her warm response, Liam asked if they could meet for breakfast. She agreed, and they decided on nine in the dining room for breakfast.

Liam had to ask a steward how he could get to the bridge and was directed to the stairs and walkway that provided access to it. When Liam walked into the doorway to the bridge, he was struck by Jamie's presence. It was clear that he was the captain. Jamie then asked Liam to join him in his captain's bridge cabin just behind the bridge. Jamie led the way to the sparse cabin used when the captain wanted to be close to the bridge and took the chair Jamie offered.

"Now tell me how you came to be on my ship, old friend?"

"It is a long story, Jamie. One that would not have been possible without you and Mr. Grogan."

"Ah, Mr. Grogan, a fine sailor and a finer man. He set me on course to becoming a captain of my own ship. With Mr. Grogan's support, I have captained four ships, each larger than the previous. Now, I am the captain of one of the fastest ocean liners in the fleet.

When we left New Orleans those many years ago, I thought I would never see you again. Tell me how you came to embark in Charleston."

For the next hour, Liam tells of his time in New Orleans without mentioning Lucy Parmenter, his time in the Army fighting the Seminole, the Mexicans, and the Indians, and finally leading a regiment in the Civil War.

"My friend, you've had many adventures. It is a wonder you have time for an ocean crossing. Where are you bound?"

"I will be taking a passage from Liverpool to Dublin and then on to my home in Knocktopher. My mother still resides there, and I hope to repay some of the kindness that allowed me to leave Ireland when I did. I owe a debt of gratitude to many."

"I hope you will be able to do that. Meanwhile, the lovely woman you asked to join us for dinner, what is your relationship with her?"

"I hope it is not too obvious, but both her beauty and her grace struck me when we first met. I have met a few women, but I am certain none compare to her. I hope during the sailing to come to know her better."

"Liam, I have been married these last twenty years to a wonderful lady. It is a blessing one should seek. So I wish you good fortune in your relationship with Mrs. Portier."

Just before nine the following day, Liam waited for Mrs. Portier at the entrance to the dining room. Her beauty and grace again struck Liam as she arrived precisely at nine, and they were shown to a table.

As they ate, Liam was taken by the quiet questions Lucinda asked and welcomed her apparent rapt interest in his story. To his delight, he saw not just a beautiful woman but a person who was interested in him for who he was. The breakfast stretched far into the morning, and both Liam and Lucinda were surprised when the maître d' quietly advised that the dining room would close for breakfast in ten minutes to reopen for lunch later. They wished to continue the conversation and moved onto the deck adjacent to the dining room. As they moved onto the deck, a bright, blue sky greeted them as they leaned forward on the railing. Each was now unwilling to break the spell cast by the sea and sky.

After what seemed like many minutes, Liam reached forward and touched Lucinda's hand,

"Mrs. Poitier, thank you for sharing a truly enjoyable dinner and morning. I enjoyed both more than ever before."

"Please call me Lucinda. I believe our relationship should be close enough that we may use our first names. And what is yours, Mr. Flaherty?"

"Liam. You did me a great favor by joining me for dinner last night and breakfast this morning. Thank you for allowing me to learn more about you. I hope we may become friends and enjoy our journey to Ireland together."

"My hope mirrors yours, Liam. You have already made this part of our journey interesting and enjoyable. Shall we share dinner again tonight?"

"Lucinda, it would give me great joy to share any meal with you."

For the nine days of the crossing, Liam and Lucinda were constant companions. During their walks along the ship's promenade deck, they shared the highs and lows of their lives. Lucinda had been married less than a month when her husband left for Virginia. She did not learn that she was a widow until months after her husband fell. Liam awkwardly tried to explain why he had never married. Lucinda suspected that sometime early in his life a woman had broken his heart. The explanation that Army life precluded opportunities was not enough.

Sharing their life experiences fashioned a relationship that promised more than each could have imagined at their first meeting. They knew the artificial environment of the ship was unlike the real world from which each came. How they might experience that world would determine how their relationship might progress. Lucinda was unaware of how things had changed in Ireland since she visited fifteen years ago. From their letters, it seemed that her grandparents remained unchanged. Liam's knowledge of Ireland was greater than Lucinda's, but only from his mother's and Father Murphy's letters. How their disparate communities might receive the two would only be known when they arrived.

An Irishman's Odyssey

Liam and Jamie Watkins often spent time together on the bridge or in Liam's cabin. Their shared experiences aboard the Primrose were frequently the topic of discussion. Both Jamie and Liam were happy that the other had successes in their life. None more so than Liam, watching Jamie perform his duties as the captain of a major ocean line. Between his time with Jamie and Lucinda, the ten days' travel across the Atlantic went swiftly by.

The travelers' arrival in Liverpool was not the end of their journey together. Liam and Lucinda had both secured passage on a ship traveling to Dublin with train connections to Queens County and County Kilkenny. The travel of a well-to-do couple in Ireland in 1868 was not unusual. Both Liam and Lucinda were now aware of the strength of their attraction to each other. By the time they were on the train from Dublin enroute to Maryborough and then on to Kilkenny Town, Liam knew he was deeply in love with Mrs. Lucinda Mayhew Poitier. He knew that this was the woman he wanted to spend the rest of his life with and that he hoped she felt the same. He believed she had strong feelings for him but might be afraid to show them. Liam didn't see their age difference as an issue. He had learned she was only thirty-one and in the prime of her life. He hoped that she did not see an issue with the age difference, for he certainly did not. As for their social status, Liam knew that the American Civil War had altered many of the social mores that had previously separated individuals. Lucinda was aware of the differences in social status between Liam and her family. She was, however, a more independent woman who, rightly or wrongly, tried to see each individual as worthwhile and unique, rather than bound by every societal construct. As the train drew near Maryborough, Liam was desperate to maintain a relationship with Lucinda and blurted out,

"Lucinda, I must see you again. There is much I want to share with you. May I call on you at your grandparents?"

"Of course. I look forward to your joining me in Maryborough and meeting my grandparents. I have their address here on this envelope. You may send me your plans to visit. I look forward to that."

When the train arrived at Maryborough, Lucinda gathered her small bag and said goodbye to Liam with a broad smile. On the platform, Liam saw Lucinda greeted warmly by an elderly man and woman. He folded the envelope from Lucinda and placed it in his pocket. The rest of the trip to Thomastown was a blur as Liam thought through possible futures, all of them including Lucinda in some fashion.

Lucinda was happy to have finally arrived at her paternal grandparents. During the carriage ride to their home, she regaled them with her time aboard the two ships with Liam. She described him as the ultimate gentleman and the type of Irishman she expected to meet in Ireland. The Mayhews were fascinated by the woman their granddaughter had become. They had not seen Lucinda since she was fifteen during her only visit to Ireland and their home. Mrs. Mayhew could tell that Lucinda was taken by Liam Flaherty. What they did not tell Lucinda was that they knew Liam as one of the heroes who fought against the Tithe Act decades ago. Having never met him, they listened intently to Lucinda's stories of their voyages together and wondered if he was the right person for their granddaughter. After all, he had been branded an outlaw for his role in the most violent opposition to the Tithe Act. Mr. Mayhew made a point to learn more about Liam Flaherty. After Lucinda was settled in her room at their home, Mr. Mayhew went to the church in Maryborough and asked Father Connor, who had moved from St Marys Church in Grannagh two decades ago, if he could learn more about Liam Flaherty. Father Connor remembered the young man he helped leave Ireland as a wanted man. After contacting Father Murphy in Knocktopher, Father Connor learned as much as he could about Liam Flaherty, since the fateful evening he had helped Liam Flaherty leave Ireland. After Mass on Sunday, Father Connor took Mr. Poitier aside and told him briefly all he had learned from Father Murphy. Although all he heard about Liam was good, Mr. Mayhew decided to say nothing to Lucinda and reserve judgment on Liam Flaherty until he had a chance to know him personally.

Liam expected that there would be no one to meet his arrival at the small Thomastown train station, so he hired a carriage to take him and his trunks the few miles to Knocktopher. He directed the carriage to the small home he remembered so well. As the carriage pulled to the gate, Liam's mother had been looking out the window and rushed out the door, exclaiming, "Praise the Lord, my boy has returned." Liam was then hugged, and his shoulder was cried upon for the next five minutes. The emotional response from his mother was not lost on Liam, and he soon found himself overwhelmed with emotion as well.

Once his trunks were carried in and placed alongside the bed, which had been just as it was when Liam left, the two sat across from each other at the small table in the kitchen and took a breath or two.

"A handsome man you are, Liam. The spitting image of your father, Aidan, God rest his soul. How long can you stay, and what can I get for you? I read your letters over and over. You have had a remarkable life since leaving Ireland. How is it you have never met and married? Surely, there have been women who found you a suitable husband."

Liam was slightly overcome by all his mother's questions and responded kindly,

"Mam, I will answer all your questions as best I can. As to how long I may stay, I do not know. I have left the Army and must decide how I will spend the remainder of my life. I have no plans other than to visit with you, see our home and the land, and visit with those I should see in the County. I owe a great debt to those who helped me so long ago. I hope to repay at least some of that.

You should know that I fell in love early in my time in America. Unfortunately, that love was not reciprocated, and I was left with a lingering heartache. It may well have soured my perspective on the women I have met over the years. Truthfully, I have had little time to myself and little time to court someone. I hope that will change, as I was encouraged by a meeting with a woman who had been on the same ships that carried me back to Ireland. She is an American and is visiting her grandparents in Queens County. I hope to continue the relationship we began during our voyage. You will find she is a wonderful woman and one to be admired. Before I tell you much more of my life in America, I want to visit some folks in the village. Where should I start?"

"I should think that Mary Nolan would welcome a visit. Michael's hanging put an end to her marriage with John Nolan. Michael is buried in the churchyard where Father Murphy remains as our parish priest."

"She and Father Murphy are on the list of those to visit. I think a visit to Michael and Father Murphy will be first. Afterward, would you like to join me in a visit to Mrs. Nolan?"

"Nay, Liam. She and I have not spoken for nigh on thirty years. She is resentful that I still have a son while she has none. It may be that your visit could temper her feelings for me."

Liam and his mother talk far into the evening and share a small dinner before Liam insists he must retire for the evening. Mary Flaherty has had many of the questions about Liam's life that were not in his letters answered. Her gratitude for his safe return knows no bounds.

Chapter 19: A Different Ireland

On a bright, sunny day, Liam walks to St. Michael's church and Father Murphy. It seems only yesterday that he snuck into the rectory seeking support from Father Murphy on what he should do after being branded an outlaw. The village of Knocktopher is not quite as he remembered. Tucked away in the gentle valley, it always seemed peaceful and unhurried during his childhood. The hills are now just as green and lush as he remembered. That is not the case with the village. As Liam looked closer at the buildings and the people walking, he was struck by an overwhelming sense of defeat. The buildings were not as well-maintained as he remembered. Some even looked as though they had been abandoned. The few people on the street seemed defeated and unwilling to meet his gaze, walking past him quickly. The village had never been like this before he left.

As the church came into view around the corner, Liam was struck by the building's disrepair and the poorly maintained graveyard surrounding the building. Liam saw an older man, slightly bent at the waist, carrying a small bundle of twigs and walking slowly to the church's side door. Liam suspects it is Father Murphy and calls out,

"Father Murphy, is it you I see tending the graves?"

With that, the man turns sharply and replies, "Indeed it is, young man. With no help from parish members, I must do what I can to keep it presentable. And who might you be haranguing me so early on a weekday morning?"

"It is Liam Flaherty, the outlaw you helped escape the hangman many years ago."

"Your letters do not do you justice, Liam. I expected a much more distinguished gentleman returning to Ireland from America."

Smiling, Father Murphy looks Liam up and down and says, Surely, you must be rich, as all Americans are these days."

"Rich, I am not. But I am willing and able to help those who helped me in my greatest time of need."

"Then, Liam, you must join me in the rectory where we may celebrate your return most appropriately. I believe I have some poitín that we can share."

Over the next two hours, accompanied by a glass or two of poitín, Father Murphy listens to Liam recount the story of his departure from Ireland, his time in the Army, and his lack of plans for the future. After Liam has finished his story, Father Murphy looks at him,

"It is no small blessing to see that a decision made many years ago was the right one. You will never know how close I came to telling you to turn yourself in to the constables that fateful night. When I learned what happened to poor Michael Nolan, I knew I had made the right choice. Your presence now speaks even more loudly about how correct I was then."

"Father, I just wanted to let you know how grateful I was then and how grateful I am now for all that you did and continue to do for our community and, of course, my mother and me."

"Young man, your letters have not done justice to your life since leaving our little village. What plans do you have now that you are no longer a member of the American Army?"

"I have not yet decided how best to proceed. I plan to spend time with my mother, make some repairs to the house, and maintain the property. I may plant some for the fall, but I have no solid plans other than visiting others. I do want to visit Michael's grave. Can you show me to it?"

"That I can. Let me put our cups up."

Father Murphy leads Liam out of the rectory and into the graveyard. Shortly, he stops in front of an ornate plaque affixed to a five-foot-tall marble pillar. Pointing to the pillar, Father Murphy smiles and says,

"When Michael was first buried, it was in a grave marked only with a small stone with his name chiseled in. After the Tithe Act was repealed and the Articles of Redemption were approved, many in Kilkenny County came together to purchase this magnificent stone and plaque in honor of Michael. All remembered the sacrifice he made to protest the unfair practice foisted upon Irishmen by the British. Michael and you are seen as the heroes of the protest movement that resulted in the repeal of the Tithe Act."

"At the time. I hardly felt like a hero, and now I wonder how our actions made that much difference. I have seen many men and a few women act heroically, and many of them, as Michael did, suffered an unwelcome death because of their actions."

"Liam, it matters not what you believe. The part you and Michael played those many years ago is remembered. If many believe what you did was important, then so be it. My only caution is that you be aware the Irish Republican Brotherhood, or the IRB, will see you as a possible leader in their campaign against British rule."

"I will proceed carefully, Father."

With a final blessing from Father Murphy, Liam walks back to his home and mother, enjoying the scenes around Knocktopher that he remembers so well. Looking even more closely at the village of his childhood, he sees how much has changed, and none of it for the better. The few Liam passes on the street keep their heads down and make no eye contact with Liam or other pedestrians. Liam notices that at least half of the shops he remembers from his youth are now closed. There is a sense of defeat everywhere in the village.

Over the next week, Liam wrote to Lucinda and asked when he might visit her in Maryborough. Her enthusiastic response within days renewed Liam's thoughts of how and when he might express his feelings for Lucinda and her response to that. A short cart ride to the train station and the train ride north to Maryborough gives Liam time to prepare his talk with Lucinda.

When the train arrives, Liam sees Lucinda alone on the platform. Her warm greeting and short kiss on his cheek are all Liam needs to know that he has not misread Lucinda's feelings toward him. On the carriage ride to her grandparents' home, Liam tells Lucinda about his return to Knocktopher, his visit with Father Murphy, and his discovery that he and Michael Nolan are considered heroes by many in Kilkenny County. While recounting his latest, he is struck again by how beautiful and vibrant the woman beside him is. He realizes he must wait until there is an opportune moment before expressing his true feelings.

Lucinda's grandparents live in a well-appointed yet unassuming home just outside Maryborough. Certainly considered wealthy by Irish standards, the house is modest in size. Lucinda leads him inside and introduces him to her grandparents. Mr. Mayhew, a vigorous man of seventy-five, smiles gently,

"So, this is the gentleman that our Lucinda cannot stop talking about?"

"Colonel Liam Flaherty is at your service, Sir," Liam says before realizing he has never used his title in front of Lucinda. Mrs. Mayhew, a solid matronly figure in an apron and bonnet, smiles knowingly at Lucinda, "An officer and a gentleman, how nice." The rising color in Lucinda's cheeks is not unnoticed.

Mrs. Mayhew is encouraged by Liam's actions and his bearing. It is clear to Mrs. Mayhew that he may have been the rebellious young man who led the demonstration against the Tithe Act, but he is now a mature, gracious gentleman. Mr. Mayhew watches Liam closely and asks,

"Colonel Flaherty, what plans have you for your time in Ireland?"

"At the moment, Sir, I have none. My mother needs support, the farm requires work, and I am indebted to many in County Kilkenny for the support they provided many years ago. I suspect it will take me more than a few months to accomplish all of these."

"It seems you do have a plan for your stay here in Ireland. Please join us for lunch."

After a leisurely luncheon served by Mrs. Mayhew, Liam and Lucinda walk the short path to the garden behind the house. Liam motions for them to sit on the small bench. He turns to Lucinda,

"Lucinda, I can no longer wait to tell you how I feel about you. You are the most wonderful woman I have ever met, and I want to spend the rest of my life with you."

"Liam, I've been waiting for this ever since we met. I feel that you and I were destined to meet, and I, too, want to spend the rest of my life with you."

"Lucinda, will you marry me?"

"I will, Liam. You have made me a happy woman this very day."

Hand in hand, the two return to the Mayhew home. Their smiling faces and shining eyes tell Mrs. Mayhew everything she needs to know. Before they can speak, she smiles, "So, I see the two of you have made some plans for your future. Are we to be part of those plans?"

"Indeed, you are, Grandmother Mayhew. Liam and I are to be married, and we hope you will be a part of that." Replies Lucinda.

Over the following weeks, Liam and Lucinda traveled between Knocktopher and Maryborough, planning a wedding that would include as many family members as possible. Liam's mother is captivated by Lucinda and often tells her that if she had a daughter, she would hope she would be like Lucinda.

Liam and Lucinda were in a quandary. Lucinda wants to get married in Charleston, her hometown, and the home of her parents. Liam wanted his mother to be at the wedding and Father Murphy to officiate. Mary initially hesitated to consider traveling to America for the wedding. On the other hand, Father Murphy was delighted to be invited, particularly when Liam told him his passage was paid for. Letters from Lucinda's parents confirmed that the Archbishop of the Cathedral in Charleston agreed to have Father Murphy be the lead priest at the wedding and finalized all the arrangements in Charleston. Liam and Lucinda arranged transport for Mary Flaherty and Father Murphy to accompany them to Charleston on a ship leaving from Dublin. Lucinda's grandparents in Maryborough were disappointed that the wedding would be held in Charleston and decided not to travel, citing age and some infirmities as the reasons. Should Liam and Lucinda return to Ireland, they insisted on hosting a reception to honor their nuptials.

Mary Flaherty and Father Murphy were enthralled with their accommodations on the ocean liner, and their first glimpse of Charleston Harbor was on a bright January morning. The meeting at the dock with Lucinda's parents was all that Liam could hope for. Mary Flaherty was greeted warmly by Mr. and Mrs. Mayhew. The warmth of their greetings swept away her initial unease. She was impressed by the stately mansion that welcomed them into its white stone walls. After being shown to her room and refreshed from the trip, she took Liam aside and asked, "Liam, are these parents of Lucinda as rich as they seem?"

"Yes, Mr. Mayhew is a well-respected person in the Charleston community and has done well."

"What may we expect at the church for your wedding? Will there be many of their friends?"

"Lucinda has limited the list of those invited to less than a hundred."

"A hundred," exclaims Mary Flaherty. "That is the entire village of Knocktopher! Have I the proper dress for such an occasion?"

"Mother, Mrs. Mayhew has a seamstress who has volunteered to accompany you to a dressmaker who will provide you with whatever you believe you need for the wedding and the gathering that follows."

In the days leading up to the wedding, Liam and Lucinda were happy to see how well their parents got along. Mr. Mayhew planned all the activities until the wedding and would host the dinner afterward. On the first day of Spring in 1869, the wedding day was bright with sunshine and the scent of honeysuckle in the gardens; Lucinda was stunning in a long, light gold gown. Dressed in his formal blue uniform, Liam looked the part of a complete officer. Father Murphy conducted the formal ceremony, joining the couple in holy matrimony, while the Archbishop performed the final consecration of their union. Sitting in the front row, Mary Flaherty could hardly control her emotions as she watched her son take his vows. His beautiful bride extended her hand for the wedding ring, which Liam gently placed on her finger. Mary was sure that if her life ended now, everything would be fine because she had never been happier than she was at that moment. The dinner party after the wedding was a whirlwind of meeting new people. Lucinda's friends admired her wedding dress and secretly envied her for the handsome officer she had married.

Unbeknownst to Mary Flaherty and the Mayhews, Liam and Lucinda planned to return to Ireland for many reasons. One of those reasons was that while they were planning the wedding and corresponding with the Mayhews, Liam and Lucinda had purchased a manor house on the outskirts of Knocktopher. During the time the new couple enjoyed their stay in Charleston, workmen labored to restore the manor house to its former glory. The other was to honor the promise made to the elder Mayhews that they would share the joy of their wedding with them in Ireland.

Liam thought the voyage back to Ireland was far too short. He and Lucinda had just discovered the joys of sex with one that each loved deeply. Ten days seemed too little for them to explore all they could share in the bedroom. Lucinda was a wonderful lover, almost equal in passion and genuine love to Liam. Too soon, the four were traveling by train and carriage back to Knocktopher. Liam and Lucinda were anxious to see what had been accomplished at their new home. Father Murphy was dropped off at the rectory with promises to see him at Mass on Sunday.

Instead of going to Mary's, Liam directed the driver to their new home. When they stopped before the imposing gate and waited for the coachman to open it, Mary looked at Liam and said, "Son, whose is this?"

"It is our new home, Mother. We hope you may join us when you feel you can no longer manage in the old home."

Mary buries her head in her hands. She is once again overwhelmed by the kindness and support from the son she thought she had lost more than thirty years ago.

Liam and Lucinda spent the following year finalizing the furnishings for their new home. Their joy in lovemaking seemed to grow almost every day. Liam enjoyed the grounds and gardens of the estate and considered himself the luckiest man alive. In the spring of 1870, Lucinda announced she was pregnant with their child. Liam was overjoyed and hurried to share the good news with his mother and

Father Murphy. A telegram to the Mayhews in Charleston was met with happiness and gratitude.

Chapter 20: A Family Legacy Grows

On a cold, blustery day in December 1870, Liam and Lucinda welcomed a baby boy. Liam asked Lucinda if she would agree to have the child named Michael Nolan Flaherty in honor of his long-lost friend. Lucinda agreed, and Father Murphy baptized Michael Nolan Flaherty the day before Christmas in St Michael's church. Martha Nolan, Michael's mother, attended the baptism and sat quietly in the back of the church while Father Murphy announced the name of Michael Nolan Flaherty and gently placed holy water on the head of the wiggling child.

Michael grew into a lively, intelligent child, deeply loved by his parents and encouraged to learn all he could about his shared ancestry. The family of three often traveled to Charleston to visit Lucinda's parents and to Maryborough to visit the Mayhews before they passed away in 1872. As their only grandchild, the Charleston Mayhews were extraordinarily generous and provided Michael with an endowment that ensured his future, wherever he chose to live and work. Liam and Lucinda enrolled Michael in the local grammar school, where he excelled academically and was recognized as an outstanding athlete.

Liam and Lucinda were happy in their new home and became substantial members of the Knocktopher community. As much as they could, they donated anonymously and generously to St Michael's Church, the local grammar school, and the Citizens Benevolent Society, which provided food and shelter to those experiencing loss.

The rehabilitation of St Michael's Church, the addition of teachers at the grammar school, and the outreach of the Citizens Benevolent Society were soon correlated with Liam's and Lucinda's arrival in Knocktopher by the more astute community members.

Liam made efforts to locate the families of Paddy Boynton, Milo Finegan, and Michael Grogan. His only success was to find a son of Milo who continued his father's poitín distribution around southern County Kilkenny. When Liam met with young Finegan, he was surprised to learn the young man was fully aware of the role his father played in Liam's departure from Ireland. Milo's role was part of their family history. Liam regretted being unable to locate any family of Michael Grogan or Paddy Boynton. Father Murphy reminded Liam that many families had left Ireland during the "Great Hunger." Grogan's and Boynton's families were likely among those that left.

In 1872, a distillery in Dublin was seeking a new location. Liam heard about the effort and approached the owners, making a convincing offer to have it in Knocktopher. The success of the new distillery and the employment it provided to the village's residents by 1874 made Knocktopher an attractive place to live and work. No longer were the shops and homes in Knocktopher ill-kept. Residents greeted each other on the streets, and the village was again a joyful place to live.

Liam's walks through the village were now far different than those he made shortly after his return three years ago. Villagers greet each other, and especially Liam. Older shops and newer shops line the main street, with many showcasing their wares in front. For Liam, this is the most apparent result of his and Lucinda's efforts to improve the lives of all their neighbors.

In 1875, the distillery owners sought to sell the property and establish another further north. Liam and Lucinda saw an opportunity and made an offer to the owners with the condition that the master distiller, Jason Baker, remain. The master distiller, pleased that the Flahertys were now the owners, assured them that he was happy in Knocktopher and would continue to provide his services to the distillery. He also suggested that the distillery undergo a name change since it was now under new ownership. Liam and Lucinda believed that the name should reflect what they felt was essential. Thus, the distillery became Cáilmheas, or goodwill in Gaelic, Irish Whisky.

By 1879, Liam and Lucinda were comfortable in their new home, firmly established as community leaders, and happier than ever in their marriage. Michael was a joy and a challenge, albeit a good one. They leveraged their good fortune wherever possible to help others while still enjoying the benefits of a comfortable life in the community.

The IRB occasionally approached Liam to join and possibly lead the effort to overturn British rule in Ireland. In each case, Liam rebuffed their offers and ignored their threats of violence. He and Lucinda were so well-respected in the community that any outsider who might bring violence to their door was quickly identified and encouraged to go elsewhere under threat of being "disappeared."

Liam's final encounter with an IRB recruiter came in the Fall of 1879. The man came to Liam's and Lucinda's home and asked to speak with Liam. The man claimed to represent the leadership of the IRB and was authorized to offer Liam a leadership position in the local branch of the IRB. Liam let the man discuss their plans and his potential role in them. He soon realized that the IRB was merely seeking Liam as a symbol of opposition to the British, based on his notoriety for opposing the Tithe. Liam's final refusal of an IRB offer was given in no uncertain terms.

"I hold no opposition to the IRB and may even find its goal a valued one. I have experienced much bloodshed over the years and will not contribute to that of fellow Irishmen. Should you in any way consider me less for not accepting your offer, be reminded that I have far more experience in the killing of men than you and will not hesitate to use it in defense of my family and myself. You may show yourself out, and I do not expect to see you or any of your compatriots ever again."

The passing of Mary Flaherty in 1881 was a solemn occasion, only brightened by the years she spent with Liam, Lucinda, and Michael before her death. Many attending her funeral had been delivered by Mary Flaherty, the midwife of Knocktopher.

Father Murphy soon followed in 1884 and was replaced by Father Donohue, the young priest who had arrived in Knocktopher in 1883. From Father Murphy, he had learned a great deal about the Flahertys and enjoyed getting to know them as stalwart members of the parish.

The eulogy Liam delivered during Father Murphy's funeral was full of anecdotes about his life and the role he played in Liam's life. Many of the younger residents of Knocktopher were unaware of Liam's role in the Tithe Act protests.

In 1888, Liam and Lucinda made the difficult decision to have Michael attend the Citadel Military College in Charleston. It wasn't easy because they knew they would see their son too little during the school year. Visits during short school breaks did not provide enough time to travel to Ireland. Michael was able to spend time with his grandparents in Charleston, and it was a joy and a blessing to them. Liam and Lucinda made plans to spend time in Charleston when they knew Michael would have time. Michael's summer visits to Ireland were planned well in advance.

1892 was a significant year for the Flaherty family. Michael graduated from the Citadel and was commissioned a Second Lieutenant of Artillery. Liam and Lucinda were among the many proud parents attending the graduation and commissioning, with Liam administering the commissioning oath to their son. The distillery, Cáilmheas Irish Whisky, which they purchased in 1885, proved to be a resounding success. That success led to the American corporation holding Jim Beam and other whisky brands, making Liam and Lucinda a purchase offer they could not refuse. The sale was made with the condition that the distillery remain in Knocktopher and retain its original name. As a result, the village and its residents continued to enjoy a quality of life that few in that part of Ireland experienced.

An Irishman's Odyssey

At 69, Liam reflected on his life and realized he had come full circle. He began his life in Knocktopher as the son of a poor farmer. His success in America and marriage to a wonderful and wealthy woman allowed him to live a gracious life in the same small village. One evening, as they often relived significant events in their lives, Lucinda urged Liam to write his memoirs and put his life experiences to paper. On the eve of his seventieth year, Liam put pen to paper. He began the chronicle of his journey from Ireland and back again—an odyssey he would have never thought possible without the care, love, and support of those he had the privilege to know in his life.

Liam finished his story in late 1895 after writing a little each day. Lucinda acted as his editor and marveled at the detail with which Liam was able to describe his many adventures. She sometimes wished she could grab Lucy Parmenter by the throat for what she did to Liam so many years ago.

Just before the turn of the century, Father Donohue delivered the eulogy for Liam Flaherty in St. Michael's Church as almost the entire village of Knocktopher attended his funeral service. Liam was extolled as a man of great accomplishment, benefaction, and leadership. His friends and neighbors would long remember his generosity and kindness. The simple headstone in the church cemetery read,

Liam Flaherty

1817-1899

Colonel, Army of the United States

Wonderful father, son, and patriot

An Irish-American of great value

May God Rest His Soul